Three Days and A Gallon of Rosé

A Novel

Dianne Zimmermann

Cover art by the author.

ISBN 978-1-950647-07-1

Publishing Assistance
BookCrafters, Parker, Colorado.
www.BookCrafters.net

*I dedicate this book to my friends
whose never-ending encouragement
drove me on when the going got tough.*

Acknowledgements

I wish to thank my family of friends for their interest and encouragement in all my writing endeavors; *Three Days and A Gallon of Rosé* is my fifth book. And I wish to express special thanks to LA Mott for her encouragement, proofreading and editing skills.

I would like to thank Suzanne Dickneite for asking on Facebook, "How did you fair in the Blizzard of '82?" I replied I was with my boyfriend in my apartment, and it was three days and a gallon of Rosé. She suggested, "I think that's the title of your next book."

Chapter One

It was in the fall of 1981 and four months before the big snowstorm was to hit the area. Dawn had just ended a romantic relationship with Dennis after they both decided that remaining good friends suited them better. Dawn was lonely and depressed and eager to meet someone new. She met Alan when she was out with her group of friends one Friday evening. They had gathered at their favorite dance place, the Panorama Lounge at the Panorama Bowling Lanes in Belleville. Dawn had been going to Panorama Lounge for years and she always enjoyed the festive atmosphere there where everyone was happy and ready to have fun dancing and meeting people. Being shy of commitment, Dawn enjoyed her safe single life void of stress and worry. Yet at times she felt lonely especially as she saw her friends pairing off into romantic relationships that led to marriage. Most of her friends, also in their thirties, were rushing to meet someone with the desire to one day settle down, get married and start a family. Dawn, on the other hand enjoyed her single life of freedom and independence because it felt safe. Panorama Lounge was like a second home to her. She was on a winter bowling league there, and each night after they finished bowling they would go into the lounge and enjoy dancing to the live music.

When Dawn was turning nineteen, her friends who were also regulars at Panorama, some of who were slightly older and of legal drinking age, always celebrated with buying several bottles of champagne for the table and the person having a birthday. Dawn's friends thought that she should have champagne too for her birthday celebration. Fred Bateman, the manager of the lounge, knew Dawn and her friends were regulars so he bent the rules a bit and sent over several bottles of champagne to their table for her birthday celebration and a good time was had by all, so they kept coming back.

Although it did not appear like it to many, Dawn was actually an introvert and did not take kindly to change or unfamiliar surroundings and adventures; but she felt at home and very comfortable at Panorama Lounge where she could come and go as she liked. Her personal freedom was behind the idea that if she drove there herself, she could come and go as she felt like it, giving her a sense of freedom, independence and control in her life.

The lounge was very popular and always so crowded that Dawn met lots of people just sitting at the end of the bar where sooner or later nearly everyone passed by her to visit the restrooms or to leave out the back way, and that was how she met Alan.

Alan tried to pass through the crowd and someone from behind bumped him, shoving him forward and splashing beer from his glass onto Dawn's front as she sat on a bar stool facing the passing crowd. He apologized profusely as she turned quickly to grab a napkin from the bar behind her. She smiled at his apologies as she began to dab the front of her blouse. They both giggled when he offered to help.

"Oh, maybe I should introduce myself first," he said with a smile. "My name is Alan."

For an instant Alan wanted to turn and thank the guy behind him for bumping into him and giving him the opportunity to apologize and meet this lovely lady who sat before him. He liked the way she looked. She was cute with an engaging smile, petite, and pretty with shoulder length blonde hair. The sage colored top she wore brought out the clear green color of her eyes that lit up when she smiled and could be seen even in the dim lights of the bar. Alan thought she appeared to be very charming; anyway, she was smiling and that was a good sign that she forgave him for spilling beer on her.

"Dawn," she responded giving her name with a smile. She wasn't a bit mad because there was something interesting about him and he seemed very nice. He had kind and expressive eyes, and as an added plus, he was tall and handsome.

"I hope that washes out," he said apologetically.

"I think it will wash out," she smiled and went on dipping the tip of the napkin in a glass of water and dabbing at her blouse to dilute the stain.

"Well, I sure hope it does wash out," Alan said and meant it.

"It was inexpensive. I got it on sale, so no big deal,"

Dawn added with a giggle. She didn't have a bra on and became a little subconscious of the wet t-shirt effect she was inadvertently creating as she nervously kept dabbing at the front of her top with the wet napkin. The dazzling sweet smile of the man standing before her was making her more nervous by the minute.

"Oh okay," he was glad to hear it wasn't really expensive.

"Although," Dawn teased when she saw that he was very concerned, "I did just buy it today, and this is the first time I have worn it." She wanted to make him feel just a wee bit guilty. She saw his smile fad a bit then. It wasn't his fault that the guy behind him wasn't paying attention and ran right into the back of him.

"Sorry," he offered. Then for hopefully extra points to impress her he added, "It looks very good on you." Alan grinned at the effective wet t-shirt look Dawn was unconsciously creating for herself.

"Thank you." She then looked down and realized how the wetness was creating a transparent top that clung to her ample breast. Realizing the look she was creating, she quickly put the napkin down and turned to retrieve her jacket from the back of the bar stool and slipped it on. Alan only smiled as she suggested the room was feeling chilly.

Alan was instantly smitten by her cuteness and perky personality. She did look very nice in the sage colored blouse with low cut neckline, exposing a bit of cleavage surrounded by the wetness, which was still revealed by the unzipped jacket.

"Please allow me to buy you a drink," he offered with a big smile, "it's the least I can do."

"Well, okay, sure," Dawn was becoming more interested in him and his kindness. He was offering to buy her a drink, and to Dawn that was the first clue that he was interested in her.

"What can I get you?" he asked.

"How about a glass of Rose, Dawn suggested. "That would be very nice." She was glad he offered and knew then he would stay and talk to her. She was pleased with a chance to talk to him more, and apparently he felt the same.

"A glass of Rose it is," he said as he motioned to the barmaid and got her attention. Enjoying their drinks and good conversation, they hung out together at the bar and talked the rest of the evening. In an effort to learn more about each other, they talked about where they grew up and where they worked. He said he was divorced, she said she had never married. They talked until they realized it was closing time. He asked her out for next evening because he was off work. When he walked her to her car he stood at her driver's side window and waited until she got her car started. He was very kind and considerate and that impressed Dawn.

The next evening he picked her up, and they went to dinner at Fischer's Restaurant then to the movie "Nine to Five" with Jane Fonda, Lily Tomlin and Dolly Parton at the Lincoln Theatre. . Alan scored points when he kidded and said he was okay to see the woman's lib movie if Dawn wanted to see it, and that it must be good since the theatre brought it back it for a second week showing. They had a few laughs when Dawn sided with the ladies in the movie and Alan sided with the outrageous womanizing chauvinistic boss played by Dabney Coleman. They laughed and discussed the movie on their drive to Panorama lounge, where they met up with Dawn's friends, Greg and Wanda, Dennis and Debbie, and Rosie and Barry. They shared drinks and conversation with lots of laugher. Dawn was glad to see that her friends took easily to Alan and that he fit in well with her group of friends.

Alan and Dawn enjoyed their date and wanted to see more of each other, so Alan suggested a dating pattern tailored to better suit their work schedules. Dawn found that although it was his idea, it worked well for her too, because she enjoyed her freedom and time to do the things she liked to do such as jog, ride her bike, and hang out with her girlfriends.

The arrangement they devised was that they would see each other on Wednesday, Friday, and Saturday evenings. He explained it was due to his shift work and the odd hours he worked as an electrician at Monsanto chemical company in East St. Louis. He was specialized in their equipment and besides working shift work he was also expected to be on call twenty-four hours a day. Dawn worked at Southwestern Bell Telephone Company as a technician in a central office in the city of St. Louis. She worked shift work and odd hours too, so they had that in common. So besides their scheduled

Wednesday, Friday, and Saturday getting together their dates were sporadic and sometimes spur of the moment fueled by the flames of desire. Alan always joked that absence makes the heart grow fonder and Dawn had to agree. In the beginning Dawn wanted more time with Alan, but soon she settled in, and got used to their routine and found that she liked it.

Chapter Two

Weeks passed and Dawn enjoyed her relationship with Alan. She was thrilled that all her friends liked Alan. Alan told everyone that he was divorced but Greg had his suspicions because Greg was unfaithful to Wanda and therefore thought he knew the signs of a fellow philanderer. Greg recognized Alan's familiar looks over the shoulder to see if any of his wife's friends were in the same restaurant or bar and the way Alan looked at other women when he was with Dawn. Alan was tall, dark and handsome and plenty of women were flirtatious.

Greg never said anything to anyone about suspecting Alan of cheating. He never said a word to Dawn and certainly not to Wanda, who couldn't keep a secret if her life depended on it. One day Greg's suspicions were confirmed as he witnessed Alan with another woman.

It was a Saturday and Greg had stopped by the home show at the St. Clair County Fairgrounds to get ideas for redoing his mother's kitchen. As he walked up and down the crowded aisles to visit the vendor booths, he thought he saw a familiar looking guy walking a few yards ahead of him. The guy looked like Alan. He was about to work his way through the crowd to approach him to say hello, but stopped short when he noticed the woman Alan was walking with and had his arm around was not Dawn. This woman had red hair that hung down from under the back of her large brimmed hat that she wore. As Greg meandered through the crowd, he daringly crept a little closer behind them. His curiosity driving him wild, he watched with the intensity of a cougar stalking his next meal. As the woman turned to talk to Alan, Greg could see that she was strikingly beautiful and made Greg's heart skip a beat; he would have gone for her himself. Greg was a little more than intrigued as he watched the two apparent lovers walk hand in hand as they looked at all the display items and spoke with distributors and contractors. Greg daringly crept up a little closer until he noticed the big shinny engagement and wedding ring set the woman wore on her left hand.

He quickly ducked out of sight behind a nearby booth partition and peeked around the partition and spied on them. He was determined not to be seen and recognized by Alan. He felt safe and out of their sight as they were busy looking at patio furniture brochures. Greg quickly searched Alan's third finger on his left hand and noticed that Alan had a wedding band on too.

Was the tall good-looking man with the gorgeous woman indeed Alan or did Alan have a twin brother? Greg thought of past conversations with Alan and could not recall Alan ever mentioning a brother, much less a twin brother. No, this guy had to be Alan; the Alan he knew who dated Dawn. Greg thought his discovery was very exciting, to find that he was not only one in their group of friends who messed around. As Greg slowly retreated and headed for the exit, he decided to keep his suspicions and what he saw to himself, for the time being.

Once outside, as Greg meandered through the large packed parking lot in search of his car, he got to thinking and realized that neither he nor any of his friends had known Alan for very long. He and Wanda had met Alan through Dawn at Panorama Lounge. They were all there when Dawn met Alan. He had only seen Alan with Dawn. Greg assumed Alan was single, as did Dawn, as did all their friends. He knew Alan did not have a twin; unless, of course, Alan lied about it; but why? Was there an estranged relationship perhaps between twin brothers who did not get along?

Greg was intrigued by his discovery, cheaters need to stick together, he thought. Besides Greg liked Alan and did not want to put him on the spot. Greg wanted to keep this secret and maybe use it to his advantage one day by holding something over Alan's head just in case he ever needed to. One thing for sure, Greg thought, things in the group of friends was going to get mighty interesting. One part of him wanted to say something to Dawn, another part of him wanted to protect Alan, so he was going to keep silent for the time being.

Chapter Three

Saturday, January 30, 1982, would prove to be a weather record-breaking day and weekend. It was the night when the big snowstorm came to town. The day started out like many other rainy days that winter. It was raining like crazy all day long and then the temperatures suddenly began to drop, and the rain turned to snow. An unexpected blizzard was about to hit Belleville, Illinois, and the St. Louis area and no one knew it was coming. A blizzard that would challenge even the most experienced road crews. The winter of 1982 would prove to be a snowplow driver's worse nightmare.

The weather people, Dawn and Alan, and their friends had no idea what was about to occur as they went on through their day's plans unknowing and unconcerned. Little did the weather bureau know to tell people that a snowstorm would dump up to twenty inches or more on Belleville that weekend, forcing schools, businesses and government offices to close, and stranding hundreds of vehicles on treacherous and impassable roadways. Everything movable was about to come to a halt.

Little did they know that even by the first day of February, officials would be reporting that Illinois 159 from Belleville to Edwardsville would be the only possible main road in the metro-east, and that Illinois Route 3 through Cahokia, Illinois, would be the only route open to St Louis. Reports came into the Illinois Department of Transportation of stranded vehicles and snow-blocked roadways.

It would get so bad out, that a woman would be giving birth in an ambulance on an Interstate 70 exit ramp near Troy, Illinois, when the ambulance got stuck on the way to the hospital. Firefighters came along and towed the ambulance to nearby Anderson Hospital. Mother and baby were reported doing fine.

The National Weather Service, which had been keeping snowfall records since 1884 reported record-breaking twenty-four-hour accumulations of over twenty inches in 1890 and fifteen inches in 1932, and Belleville may have had similar measurements. Road crews were not prepared for this large amount of snow and everything shut down, and by February 9, 1982, highway workers would still struggle. They didn't know there would be nearly thirty days of snow plowing spread out from the end of January and through February.

Records showed in later years stories told by the snowplow crews that it seemed like every third or fourth day it would snow again and that some snows were significant enough to take two or three days to clear roadways, and then it would snow again. It seemed like the equipment went non-stop. Equipment was wearing out and breaking down. There were huge snowdrifts, some up to ten feet high around Belleville. Highway maintenance crews resorted to special equipment like backhoes, high lifts and graders to clear the roads. They had to load snow onto trucks and haul it away instead of plowing it to the side.

Stranded motorists packed hotels and stayed in temporary shelters at fire and police stations, schools, community centers and truck stops. The extreme snowfall wreaked havoc in all areas. Roofs were caving in from the heavy weight of the snow. Store supplies could not keep up with demands and ran out of tire chains, rock salt, snow shovels, milk, bread and eggs. Surprising officials reported no serious accidents or injuries, but several men died of heart attacks while walking in deep snow, shoveling or driving in dangerous conditions.

Tempers rose as people were cooped up for days so domestic violence occurred. There were reports of drivers taking nearly six hours to go sixty miles from Springfield to New Douglas and three hours to go fifteen miles from New Douglas to Troy, Illinois. It was just a chaotic time that lasted too long and began to work on people's nerves.

Chapter Four

Along with everyone else in the Metro-East, Alan and Dawn, had no idea of what was to come and that the heavy rains would change to a huge blizzard as the temperatures dropped throughout the afternoon. They had plans to do something together that Saturday evening. Alan had met up with Greg in the afternoon to play racquet ball then have a few beers afterward. Greg invited Alan and Dawn over for dinner at his apartment that evening. Alan called Dawn to let her know and confirm that it was okay with her. He called and was happy to find her at home. He was always happy to hear her cheerful voice.

"Hey, what's up," she asked, glad he called.

"Hi, I'm at Tim and Joe's with Greg," Alan held the payphone receiver closer to his ear and spoke loud above the noise of the crowded bar.

"Oh, you are," commented Dawn.

"I owed him a beer after he won all three games we played. He and Wanda just invited us over for dinner this evening," urged Alan.

"Oh, they did," Dawn was pleased to hear about the invite.

"How does that sound to you," asked Alan?

"Sounds fun," answered Dawn. She liked Greg and Wanda. Greg was a jokester and always came up with clever wise-cracks even if it was usually at the expense of women; they liked the dumb blonde jokes, or jokes about trading in their two women sitting in the backseat of the car for the two younger ones they saw walking down the sidewalk as they drove past them. Wanda would just roll her eyes and Dawn chuckled at the silly guy jokes.

Watching Greg and Alan interact at Dawn and Wanda's expense always made Dawn laugh when she thought that most women would be mad. Dawn got a kick out of Greg and Wanda's humor too. They were a handsome couple and had dated for several years. Wanda, lived at home with her mom and dad officially, but gradually moved more and more of her things into Greg's apartment. She slept there more times than not, until it was determined by everyone, if not fully admitted by Greg, that they lived together. Wanda had great taste and decorated Greg's apartment. She was the epitome of the latest styles and fashions. She dressed Greg too, you could easily tell that as their outfits always matched. They made a handsome couple. He was tall and good looking and she a blue-eyed-blonde, with a splattering of freckles across her nose and cheeks, lots of curly hair and a lovely smile.

"I'll come by then at four, if that time works okay for you," Alan said.

"Sounds great," answered Dawn, but then thought

of the weather forecast she had just heard on the radio about the rain possibly turning to a light snow with some accumulation.

"Wait, are you sure we should go?" Dawn was a little concerned. "I would love to see Greg and Wanda, but I just heard an updated forecast, and they are saying now that the rain is supposed to turn to snow, possibly two to three inches this evening."

"Oh, what's a little snow?" joked Greg who was eavesdropping in the background and egged Alan on. Dawn could hear him and smiled.

"I think we'll be okay," encouraged Alan as he thought of his little yellow Volkswagen and was eager to drive it in the snow.

"Are you sure?" Dawn asked kiddingly.

"I think we'll be fine," Alan replied and then quickly added, "My little Volkswagen sits up high, has the engine in the rear over the drive wheels, and the narrow wheels will easily go through snow." Alan was so proud of his 1976 Yellow Volkswagen Bug and couldn't wait to get out in the snow with it.

"If you're sure," laughed Dawn, enjoying Alan's humor and eagerness to get together. She was eager to see him.

"Hey, a Volkswagen is what the snowplow driver drives in order to get to the snowplow." He laughed.

Alan lived in Villa Hills about ten miles away from where Dawn's apartment was located. As it was, he and Greg were already four miles closer to Dawn's apartment since they were having beers at Tim and

Joe's, on West Main. They were making the rounds and had just left Jimmy Connor's Center Court bar and restaurant down the street. Belleville was proud of their native-born star tennis player, Jimmy Connor. Alan and Greg had stopped at the bar hoping to get a glimpse of the tennis star. He wasn't there of course, but they enjoyed looking at all the pictures and sports memorabilia displayed on all the walls. Alan liked the place and promised to take Dawn there for dinner one evening.

Chapter Five

Dawn liked her and Alan's dating arrangement by which they saw each other only two or three times a week. This arrangement gave Dawn lots of freedom to hang out with her girlfriends. Dawn loved spending time with her friends especially one on one time with her best friend Nancy. Dawn had a secret crush on Nancy. Nancy was wild and crazy and flirted with her and everyone else. Whenever Nancy was free and in between dates or boyfriends she would call Dawn to hang out together. They would go shopping or visit her aunt and uncle who lived about twenty miles south down Route 158 to Route 3 into Waterloo, Illinois.

Dawn's early Friday evenings and Saturday afternoons were for Nancy, as Alan usually worked early Friday evenings and then hit the bars with his buddies on Saturday afternoons. Saturday nights were saved for Alan and Dawn to be together.

Dawn eagerly looked forward to seeing Alan, he was a lot of fun and they enjoyed each other's company no matter if they went out or stayed in for an evening alone. Alan always came to Dawn's apartment; she never went to see him at his place. She had never been to Alan's place, not once since they began dating. Alan always picked her up or he would meet her at the Panorama Lounge which was now their special place to meet.

Dawn wasn't sure whose company she enjoyed more, Nancy's or Alan's. With Alan, she felt feminine and felt that she fit in with all the couples they hung out with, but she secretly had a crush on Nancy. Was that normal she wondered? It was grand to be dating a tall handsome guy, all the ladies looked up to and the guys in the group easily got along with. Dawn not only felt feminine being with Alan, but also accepted that only straight couples fit into social norms.

Living the straight life would be easy if only for appearances sake; but there was another side to Dawn, the real side, the side she tried to ignore but could not ignore—her heart ached for something she knew she would never have. She could not be married to a man for that reason, for that would not be honest, so she had no desire to get married. She enjoyed her freedom, which was important to her. Down deep she desired a relationship with a woman knowing all too well that it would never be, because she was attracted to straight women.

Dawn ached for the warm loving touch of a woman. It was what Dawn's heart longed for, and so a void was left in her heart never to be fulfilled. To Dawn, loving a woman was total love: heart, body, mind and soul. And of course, sex not as satisfying with a man as she knew it could be, as it was in her dreams with a lovely woman partner. So Alan was her socially acceptable man even though at times her heart ached for who she knew she would never have, Nancy. Sometimes she wished she never felt the way she did; but there was just something about Nancy that rocked her soul and stole her heart.

Dawn was deeply troubled by her feelings for another woman that were stronger than her feelings for a man. She thought she was the only woman in Belleville, Illinois, who had a crush on another woman. She could never bring herself to talk about it to anyone for fear as seeming weird and being ostracized from her group of friends. She wondered if her fascination with unobtainable Nancy was a way to distance herself from formal commitment to Alan. Dawn's childhood felt rather loveless to her, as her home life was tumultuous. Her parents fought all the time. Her mother was cold, her father distant, argumentative and the discipline and orders he barked were strict and unforgiving. She remembered at about age twelve saying she was never going to get married and her mother snapped, "You're supposed to," which just fortified Dawn determination not to marry and to stay single.

Dawn kept her feelings toward Nancy to herself. She feared the consequences of being rejected by both Alan and Nancy if they found out. She felt terribly alone in her predicament. She felt she had no one to talk to about it. Dawn had never been to a psychologist, but she felt so stressed about her emotions that she felt that she had to talk to someone about her situation. She was tormented to the point where she finally made an appointment with a therapist. She had never gone to a psychologist before and so she just picked a name from the list of those provided on her work insurance plan.

Dawn dreaded the upcoming appointment. She hated talking about herself and being the center of attention. As a child she was brought up to be quiet until you are spoken to. The day of the appointment finally came. She wished she had cancelled it, but she didn't, so she decided to go. The appointment was strenuous and turned out to be a weird experience that got her nowhere in the way of coming to an understanding of why she felt the way she did.

Dawn thought the psychologist seemed very uncomfortable when she brought up the subject that maybe she was gay. She wondered if maybe he was very religious or a latent homosexual himself, because he skirted around the whole gay, lesbian issue when she brought it up. She felt uncomfortable, which made her reason to why she made the appointment feel very weird. It was apparent to her that he wanted to avoid the whole gay issue because he simply began talking about his wife and kids.

Dawn thought that was rude, embarrassing and weird, and vowed never to visit another psychologist regarding the issue, and so her pain and confusion lived on. She tried to figure out her feelings herself wondering if she felt that way about woman because her mother was distance and cold, as was her father.

"Come on Dawn, it will be fun, I'll be over by four," coaxed Alan. Alan always gave himself a little extra time to get to Dawn's apartment so he could stop at every bar along the way on Main Street. And the city of Belleville had one of the longest main streets in the country that ran east to west for over ten miles.

Belleville was an old German community were most of the immigrants were small farmers, brew masters at the brewery, or they worked in the underground coal mine shafts. The shaft mines were abandoned now and only parts of rusting deteriorating metal buildings remained behind and reminded the local residents of their past existence. Although through the years the old abandoned mine shafts wreaked havoc in the town of Belleville reminding residents of the distant past in the form of sinkholes and sinking houses.

In more recent times big corporate coal extracting companies such as Peabody Coal Company, used the surface mining method, called strip miring, in lieu of underground mine shaft mining. It was easier and cheaper for coal companies because they just striped away soil and rock to get access to the coal. But lots of farmland was forever destroyed when sold for coal mining purposes. Peabody promised when they were through mining the land, the land would be smoothed out and made useable again. Those promises were not kept. Instead many acres of farmland surrounding communities such as Freeburg, Smithton, and Milstadt were left very rocky and hilly with deep drop-offs into pits.

The land was rendered useless for farming and even for grazing cattle. The torn-up land was too rocky with steep hills and pits that were too dangerous for cattle to roam and graze. After stripping the topsoil and mining all the coal deep holes were left that filled up with water and were also rendered too dangerous for recreational purposes. "No swimming" signs were posted only to be ignored on tempting hot summer days. The lakes had unpredictable drop offs and dangerous depths, but swimmers ignored the warning signs and went swimming anyway only for some to tragically drown.

Besides coal mining, Belleville's German population was also a beer brewing community. Stag brewery was established in 1850 and was still productive in 1982. Also popular was Falstaff beer brewed on the banks of the Mississippi in St. Louis which employed hundreds of people. However, the largest brewery was located up the street from the Falstaff brewery and it was called Anheuser Busch Brewery, which was established by German immigrants back in the early 1800s.

What made Anheuser Busch unique and popular in the metro St. Louis area was that it sponsored taverns. A corner tavern could be found on many neighborhood city blocks in the city of St. Louis and in Belleville. It was Anheuser Busch who had the genius to introduce the corner tavern. They built the brick buildings to host the taverns on the first floor with living quarters on the second floor for the owner-managers. And the brewery provided the giant neon Anheuser Busch signs with the famous flying eagle emblem. The signs were placed right above the tavern door angled to face the street corner to be seen from all directions-thus the name, the corner tavern.

Alan regularly visited a few of those corner taverns usually on his way to Dawn's apartment. He would have a quick beer and chat with his favorite barmaids. All the barmaids knew Alan by name, Dawn was jealous when she had the rare honor of accompanying him one day as they were out and about and made several tavern stops. Alan was tall and good-looking, and all the ladies told him so which fed his super ego. Dawn was jealous when they flirted with him, secretly she wished they flirted with her too. But today, he and Greg were making the rounds together and having a high ole time. So when Alan arrived at Dawn's apartment at four in the afternoon he was a little tipsy and ready for a quickie.

Dawn's apartment was located on George Street, a dead-end street off of E. Adams Street. Her apartment was a short walk if you cut-through a driveway over to Mascoutah Avenue. Dawn apartment was on the end in one of the one-story brick buildings that made up the complex. There were plenty of parking spaces in the back of the long buildings housing six apartments each. Dawn was happy there, as it was a step up for her.

It was Dawn's first nice apartment after she got a union job at the phone company which paid well, so she could afford to rent a nicer place. That was after she upgraded and transferred from a clerk status to a man's job title, Communications Technician status. She was initially passed up for the transfer, so the union steward helped with the matter and she got the higher paying job.

She was happy and thinking about her good fortune when she had heard Alan's Volkswagen pull around her unit and park in the back. It had already begun to snow, and she hurried to the back of the building to unlock the bedroom patio door to let him in so he would not have walk around to the front door.

"Hey, there you are," greeted Dawn as she opened the patio door.

"Hey there," he grinned as she opened the patio door. He stomped his snowy shoes on the outside doormat, and she brushed the scattering of snowflakes off his shoulders before he leaned down to kiss her. The kiss was long and inviting.

"Hi there yourself," she managed to smile and look into his eyes before he kissed her again.

"Oh, how convenient." He glanced around the bedroom. They giggled as he danced her back to the bed and gently laid her down, kissing her as he unbuttoned her top.

"We are going to be late," acknowledged Dawn with a giggle in her voice glancing at her watch. But she really didn't care if they were a little late arriving at Greg and Wanda's.

"Oh, they won't mind," Alan managed to whisper between deep kisses. Just then they were startled and jumped, then giggled even more as the wall phone near the kitchen rang its loud thrilling ring.

"I bet that's Wanda calling," said Dawn, "she's probably calling to remind me to bring the bottle of wine I said I would bring."

"We better get going," Alan said almost begrudgingly. Suddenly lying there together on the bed felt so cozy as he pulled her close.

"Don't let me forget the wine." Dawn ordered as she snuggled closer to Alan underneath the warm covers.

"I won't, I promise," assured Alan with a smile then kissed her gently. He was well aware Dawn had a habit of forgetting things if she didn't use those clever yellow Post-It notes and leave them in plain sight all over her apartment.

Dawn had a glass or two of wine while waiting for Alan to get to her place, so their sexual escapade was more about laugher than actual sex on this snowy evening. They were both so warm and cozy that they could have just stayed there in bed.

"Okay, for real this time, we better get going," said Dawn reluctantly rising up from the bed. She slipped on her sweater, jeans and boots and grabbed her hat, coat, scarf and gloves and the bottle of wine and off they went in Alan little yellow Volkswagen.

Chapter Four

Little did Dawn and Alan realize that they were driving into what may turn out to be the biggest snowstorm to hit the area in decades. They had no idea that the next day, Sunday, January 31, 1982, *Belleville News Democrat* would report the event in detail calling it the blizzard they missed reporting. A mere four inches was predicted, but the weatherman got it all wrong when the weather pattern stalled over the Metro-East area. The four inches predicted easily turned into an eighteen to twenty-four-inch blizzard that would go down in history as the biggest snowstorm since 1932 to hit the area.

It would be a snowplow driver's nightmare the *News Democrat* would report the next day. Schools would be closed, and hundreds of vehicles would be stranded on treacherous roadways. Businesses were encouraged to close and tell employees to stay home. It was predicted that the snowdrifts could get up to ten to twelve feet high. Special equipment such as backhoes, high lifts and graders would be needed to clear roads. Snow would be loaded on to trucks and then on to train cars and hauled away instead of plowing it to the sides of the roads and streets.

There was an all-out warning that the weight of the heavy snow could cause many roofs to collapse. People could become concerned as stores ran out of tire chains, snow shovels, and the usual substantial basic supplements such as milk, bread and eggs. There were warnings that babies may be born in cars trying to get to the hospital and people asphyxiated sitting in vehicles with the motors running to keep warm while stuck in snowdrifts. It was warned that men of all ages and health conditions could experience heart attacks from shoveling snow. It was a concern to authorities that people cooped up together would probably get on each other's nerves and that domestic violence would explode and that sick or injured people could die because ambulances could not get to them. And so were the warnings and predictions put out by the news media.

Chapter Five

Snow was beginning to fall as they drove to Greg and Wanda's apartment complex on Roger Street off of Kinsella Avenue in Swansea, which was about a five-mile drive from Nancy's apartment. Snowfall was becoming heavier as they pulled up to Greg and Wanda's apartment parking area. Greg met them at the door with a warm smile.

"Nice night isn't it?" Greg greeted them ready to party as Alan handed him the bottle of wine he and Dawn brought with them.

"Ah, Rosé, our favorite," Greg laughed, thinking how Wanda lovedRosé and would have this bottle emptied in no time.

Samantha, their small whippet dog, barked two friendly barks in greeting to the couple and then went to curl up on her doggie bed near the fireplace in the living room to avoid the cold breeze and snowflakes that drifted in before Greg could close the door.

"Come in here," Wanda called from the kitchen, "so we can talk while I cook." She was elbow deep into pots and pans, spoons and bowls and sported splashes of fresh spaghetti sauce on her bib apron. Wanda was known for physically getting into her cooking; she knew it and would readily agree she was sloppy. There was sauce splattered on the front of her apron and in her hair. Several dirty pots and pans were stacked on the kitchen counter and some were soaking in the sink.

"Sure smells good," Dawn said as she entered the kitchen. Wanda gave her a quick hug and patted her back with one hand as she continued to stir the pot of sauce with her other hand. Wanda and Dawn kept their distance to not get greasy lasagna sauce drippings from Wanda's apron on Dawn's light blue sweater.

Wanda smiled at Greg and made nice; she was determined to forget, for now anyway, the snide remarks he made about her flirting with Alan at every opportunity. Before they arrived, Greg reminded Wanda that it was she who suggested they invite Alan and Dawn over for dinner. And that was true, because she wanted to see if Dawn flirted with Greg, but little did she realize Greg wanted to see if Wanda flirted with Alan. Wanda suspected Greg and Dawn of having an affair. Wanda was suspicious because she was secretly attracted to Alan. Their jealousies consumed their individual imaginations and to each their own tormented versions of Peyton Place.

The dinner was accompanied by lots of wine. The first serving was Caesar salad, served with garlic cheese bread. The delicious fresh vegetable garden salad and piping-hot garlic cheese bread alone was enough to fill up Dawn. She unbuttoned the top button of her pants to make room for more as Wanda began dishing out the lasagna. Dawn had been starving herself all week so she could get into her tight-fitting skinny jeans. Dawn feared another week of starvation was in her future.

The more Greg and Alan drank, the more intense the conversation regarding relationships became. Dawn thought Greg was acting a little weird, as if he knew a secret about Alan. They snickered at sly jokes about shift work and never being home.

Working shift work had its advantages besides getting the extra differential pay that Greg, Alan and even Dawn earned through their various individual union contract negotiations. All three were grateful, especially Dawn, a woman finally in what was always considered to be an unattainable better paying man's job at the phone company. Nixon signed the 1970 Title Nine Act for women to get more funding and more opportunity in sports in schools, and Johnson had signed the Affirmative Action Bill that President Kennedy introduced in 1963 for women and minorities to address the long histories of discrimination faced by minorities and women. It was now their time for opportunities to get better paying jobs; jobs that were formerly only considered to be men's jobs.

Dawn was very grateful for the opportunity to make better pay like the men made. Wanda was a dental hygienist and the only one of the four who worked a non-union job. She was happy to have regular daytime hours but was not so happy about her low pay.

Wanda was a great cook and served up a much-anticipated tasty dish of Lasagna. Even though Dawn was already full, she could not resist the flavorful aromas that had been permeating throughout the apartment. It was delicious and she ate too much as usual and had to unzip her pants. She was reminded again, for one depressing moment, that she would have to starve herself for the rest of the week. She did not mind dieting because it would be worth Alan telling her how cute she looked, so nice and slender in her jeans. She always loved his compliments, which were always great dieting incentives for her. She liked it too when she felt thinner and did not have to fight to squeeze into her jeans and get them zipped up and buttoned.

"How about another serving of Lasagna," Wanda offered, "don't forget, there is more garlic bread."

It was quite evident to Dawn that Wanda came from a very large family and was used to cooking for lots of people because she had prepared a lot of food.

"I am stuffed," sighed Alan, "it was so delicious. I wish I could eat more." He added pushing himself back from the table. Dawn and Greg easily followed suit, pushing back their chairs and sighing, feeling very stuffed, and they all laughed.

"Is everyone ready for dessert," asked Wanda watching their faces grimace in obvious discomfort. "It's sorbet, very light sorbet."

"There's always room for sorbet," announced Greg as he mimicked the popular television Jell-O commercial.

"Come on, let's sit in the living room by the fireplace and have our dessert," suggested Wanda.

They all settled on the sofa and wing back chairs

near the warmth of the blazing fireplace. Greg added logs, stirred, and poked until it flared up and heated the whole apartment.

"What the hell you trying to do" asked Wanda with big eyes and a sarcastic tone, "melt my sorbet?" Everyone laughed, as they were all getting drunk on wine and sugar.

"Sorbet," whispered Alan in Dawn's ear, "I'm glad it's nice and light, I'm stuffed." He laughed and rubbed his stomach which protruded over his gapped unbuttoned pants. They both were feeling light-headed as the wine and sugar took effect. Dawn knew the wine was going to Alan's head, and she only smiled and poked him in the ribs when Wanda stepped back into the kitchen and Greg was tending the fire. Alan leaned over and kissed her.

"I'm stuffed too. I can barely breathe," she laughed.

Wanda walked back into the living room when a flash of light and a loud boom brought them all to their feet. They all jumped in surprise hearing a loud bang and seeing a flash that lit up the dark sky and the whole parking lot.

"Wow, what was that?" asked Wanda.

"Did a streetlight just blow?" Dawn wondered in amazement. She had never seen a streetlight blow before. She thought that maybe lightning struck it.

"I think that was thunder and lightning," insisted Greg.

"What," remarked Wanda, "you must be kidding," She, along with the others, had never heard thunder and saw lightning while it was snowing. They looked at each other in amazement and gathered at the front window to get a better look.

"My god, look how hard it is snowing now," remarked Alan. Big flakes were raining down. The snow looked heavy and was coming straight down like thick rain.

"I have never experienced thunder and lightning while it was snowing," said Dawn looking around at the wide-eyed looks of wonder as they all looked out the front windows.

"This is my first, babe," Alan confessed as he pulled Dawn close to him and smiled down at her and kissed her head affectionately.

"This is my first!" Wanda commented looking at the others in amazement.

"I can't believe this," exclaimed Dawn with a bit of a concerned sound to her voice, along with her excitement. The air was electric and they could feel the charge linger in the moist night air as they stepped outside on the walkway to have a better look. The wonder of nature was fascinating but could be very eerie at the same time.

"Wow, I think we are really going to get it now," said Alan with a tone of excitement as it began to snow even heavier. Alan stepped out further and looked to see how deep the snow was getting in the parking lot, in seconds he was covered with blowing snow. Suddenly he became excited and was eager to see how his Volkswagen would do in deep snow.

"I think we better get going," suggested Dawn

looking around at the thick flakes falling almost like rain all over them. It didn't take long before they were covered in a white blanket of snow.

"I think you are right," agreed Alan, "it's best we get going."

"It's like a blizzard out here," pointed out Greg. Big flakes were blowing so thick they couldn't see beyond a few yards across the parking area.

"You are welcome to stay the night," offered Wanda gazing at Alan with a teasing smile feeling the five big glasses of wine she had throughout the evening. She laughed as Alan winked at her but then quickly turned his attention back to Dawn. He looked at Dawn, as if to say, if we are going to leave, we better get going now.

"Greg and Wanda, thanks for a wonderful evening. Dinner was delicious," Alan said, and Dawn agreed as they turned to go back inside.

"We'll just finish our desserts then we better get going," suggested Alan.

"Yes, we can't leave without finishing this delicious sorbet," confessed Dawn and with two big spoonfuls she and Alan were both finished with their deserts. The weather was making her nervous, but the desert was delicious and went down easily.

"I think we better get going, now for sure," suggested Alan again and Dawn agreed. Alan was concerned, and Dawn seeing the worried look on his face was becoming more concerned herself. She thought Alan's Volkswagen would be good in the snow, but the drive home was sure to be challenging. It was apparent that as hard as it was snowing it was going to get deep, and the little Volkswagen was only good for about eleven inches of snow before the car would be too low to clear the snow and get stuck and buried.

They finished their last teaspoons of sordid and last sips of coffee, as they listened to Phil Collins sing "In the Air Tonight."

"What an appropriate song for this night," pointed out Wanda looking at the others and they all had to agree.

All of a sudden, they heard another thunderclap and saw a flash of lightning. They all looked at each other with wide eyes of amazement. They knew they would not forget this evening for a very long time, and it would be added to the list of remarkable "where were you when" events such as when President John F. Kennedy was assassinated and the landing on the moon took place. They knew that in the years to come, people would ask: "Where were you and what were you doing during the big snow blizzard of 1982?"

"We better get going if we are going to go at all," repeated Alan seeing the flirting smile slowly grow on Wanda face breaking down his wine weakened resistance. Wanda winked and Alan quickly looked at Dawn and added, "Don't you think we should head out?"

"Yes, I do," Dawn agreed. She was actually becoming concerned in an excited fun way. It was going to be an exciting ride home. There was something very exciting about hearing thunder and seeing high lightning flash across the night sky as big flakes came raining down in thick waves. I was bound to be a night to remember for a long, long time.

Greg hurriedly went to the closet and got their things and handed Alan and Dawn their coats, hats, and gloves and scarves. Dawn was glad she wore her high boots with good gripping tread on the soles. They were comfortable, fleece lined, and nice and warm. Just what she needed in this bazaar blizzard that they were witnessing.

Quick hugs were given all around and Alan and Dawn thanked Greg and Wanda once again for the lovely time as they headed out the door to the car.

"Wanda and I will help clear off your car," offered Greg and he and Wanda quickly bundled up and went out to brush the snow off Alan's car. It only took a minute with the four of them working to clear the little Volkswagen of deep snow. But the snow was coming down so fast with big flakes that it could have been a continuous job because as quickly as they cleared it off, it was covered up with snow again. They all had to laugh at their endless seemingly useless efforts.

"We can't keep up with it," laughed Wanda sounding out of breath.

"We will just have to manage as best as we can," said Alan as he and Dawn quickly climbed into the car and hurriedly closed the doors to keep the snow from flying inside the car. Alan had no trouble getting the car moving when he shifted into reverse. He backed up a bit, stopped and called out to the others.

"So far so good," Alan shouted and laughed from the open driver side window as snow flew in his face. The snow instantly dotted his hair and beard. He had to blink his eyes as snowflakes were landing on his eyelashes. He stopped then quickly pushed in the clutch and shifted the little car into first gear letting the clutch slowly out as he mentally hoped for the best as did Greg and Wanda who were standing by watching closely.

They all cheered when the car began to lurch forward. The little yellow bug labored along, front wheels sliding a bit to the side, but the rear drive wheels under the weight of the engine gripped the snow very well. Dawn held her breath and Greg and Wanda stood and watched with hope that Alan and Dawn would make it home okay. Alan steered slightly left to head up and out of the parking lot. Dawn rolled down her window to wave and say good-bye to Greg and Wanda, and they waved back.

"Wave for me," Alan requested, he was too busy, shifting then steering with his right hand as he used his left hand to reach out and around the open driver-side window to brush snow from laboring wipers that struggled to clear the windshield. Seeing was one thing, hoping to keep the car moving through the ever-deepening snow was another concern. Having the weight of the engine in the back helped, but still the back wheels slipped a bit. Steering was tough because the front end wanted to raise up a bit and go another direction rather than where Greg was steering and that felt scary to both of them. It was a bit of a struggle; they were slipping and sliding. Neither one said a word rather they were concentrating as hard as they could as if their prayers and positive thoughts alone would get them up the hill.

Chapter Six

They breathed a sigh, when much to their relief; they finally made it up the little hill out of the parking area to the street okay and did not slide into the ditch. Alan honked a good-bye to Greg and Wanda who were standing near their door still watching their little yellow car struggle through the ever-deepening snow.

"I'm going to run this stop sign," Alan announced as he pulled up to Roger Street.

"Sounds like a good plan to me," encouraged Dawn looking in both directions.

"No one is coming anyway, and I'm afraid I won't get going again if I dare to stop," Alan said with a serious tone to his voice as he carefully pressed on the gas and shifted into second gear while making the turn.

"We are still moving and that is what counts," Dawn was worried but thought it all so exciting. She had never seen it snow like this before. It was surreal and beautiful. She was in awe of her first thunder snow experience. She felt for sure that this was going to be a record snowfall for the Belleville area.

They managed the two rather steep hills on Kinsella Avenue and then turned cautiously onto Gilbert Street.

Alan was cautious and drove slowly, careful not to make any sudden moves while steering or braking. Carefully they made their way east to North Illinois Street, where they ran that stop sign and turned right to head south toward the round-about fountain that everyone referred to as the "Square" in downtown Belleville. The car struggled a bit, but they moved along okay as they headed south on North Illinois Street. Alan thought that going around the square then heading east on East Main, and making a right turn then on Mascoutah Avenue, would be the best way to go to avoid any steep hills and Dawn agreed. They were concerned but both were in awe and enjoyed the view of the beautiful very silent and serene snowy night. It was a winter wonderland. The heavy snow acted as a sort of insulation causing the night air to be very quiet except for the laboring sounds of the little Volkswagen's engine behind them that struggled to turn the wheels through the thickening snow. They looked around and realized that they were the only ones on the roadways. Feeling a little foolish to be out there, Alan drove slow and very carefully.

"Are we nuts?" exclaimed Alan. "We are the only ones out here on the streets."

"Too late now, we are out here," Dawn reasoned but sounded worried.

"I'm going to run this red light," he announced looking in both directions and feeling secure that no one was coming through the intersection. He was afraid to stop and lose their momentum for fear that they wouldn't be able to get going again. There were no cars anywhere in sight, reminding them again that they were the only nuts out on the streets. Evidently every other citizen in the area yielded to the weatherman's warnings and knew to stay off the roads.

"Running the red lights sounds like a great idea to me," agreed Dawn as she looked in all directions as they ran the red lights and drove through the intersections. There was excitement in the air by the thunder and heavy snowfall and the thought of running stop signs and red traffic lights. They assumed that surely any police officer would go along with that idea under these unusual conditions.

Besides, they were the only visible moving headlights shinning on the silent, so quiet it was deafening winter wonderland that enveloped the landscape. It was beautiful, electrically charged and magical. It seemed to them rather sad that they were the only ones out there taking it all in. Dawn turned the radio on only to hear winter weather advisory and road conditions. The radio announcer on the local station suggested everyone stay off the roads so when snowplow drivers are able to get to their equipment, they can clear the streets without too many abandoned stuck vehicles getting in their way. According to the radio announcer, more snow was on the way and that it may be days before anyone could get out and drive on the roads. Walking was preferred and heavily suggested if anyone was going to get out at all and they were even cautioned against that. Just stay in and keep warm, they suggested.

The little Volkswagen rear engine seemed alive as it roared its determination from behind them. Silently they each listened and sometimes held their breath when they thought the little motor would sputter and die. Alan and Dawn both praised its powerful drive and seemingly tenaciousness to keep trudging through the snow. They could see that the snow was getting deeper on the streets. The way the little Volkswagen's engine struggled Alan guessed the snow was getting as deep as the front bumper and soon they would be pushing snow instead of driving through it. If that were to happen, they would have to abandon the car and walk the rest of the way to Dawn's apartment which was about a mile further. They only hoped and prayed that they could keep going until they reached her apartment. They looked in all directions at intersections and saw that they were the only car on the street. They suddenly realized that they might be considered to be crazy for even being out there.

"Are we crazy?" laughed Alan filled with wonder and adventure and loving it.

"We are the only ones out here," agree Dawn pointing out the obvious while looking around, "what does that tell you?" And Alan laughed along with her. They were feeling pretty confident just as long as the little determined Volkswagen labored on. Alan and Dawn's eyes grew large with wonder as they looked at each other. The little engine behind them chugged along pushing the little car through the snow. So far so good! Miraculously the little skinny tires somehow continued to grip the snow and plow through it.

"I'm so glad that I bought new tires last month," Alan said thinking new deep tread surely had to help.

"I bet there is at least fifteen inches on the streets already," exclaimed Dawn.

"I can't believe this!" Alan laughed in amazement along with Dawn, as he reached in his pocket and pulled out his handkerchief and used it to wipe clear the fogged up windshield in front of him and then handed it to Dawn so she could clear her side.

This was surely turning out to be an occasion they would never forget when years later when someone would ask the question: "Where were you in the blizzard of '82?"

"This much snow was certainly not predicted," said Dawn, "this is a crazy blizzard."

Just then there was another thunderclap and lightning strike and they both squealed and jumped in their seats, then looked at each other and laughed.

"Wow! That sounded close," yelled Dawn and Alan laughed.

"Look taillights," exclaimed Alan as he watched them in the distance ahead of them turn out on to East Main.

When Alan got to that intersection where the truck turned out in front of them onto the street, he tried to drive in the quickly fading tire tracks. But the tracks were filling up fast due to the heavy snowfall and lack of traffic. The semi-truck left a nice packed groove for them to drive in. They were quiet now as they carefully traveled on East Main Street. It was a private winter wonderland, just for them. The city's snow-covered beauty being reflected in the steady street light glare.

They slowly drove a few blocks east and held their breath when they had to make the somewhat slanted uphill right turn onto Mascoutah Avenue. They slipped and fishtailed a bit on the incline. It was just enough that they felt the rear wheels fail to grip. They were getting there; they were close, only about a half mile from Dawn's apartment. So even if they had to walk the rest of the way, they could do it and they would be okay. Although they knew it would be best to get the car to her place and off the street, otherwise it would be completely buried by snowplows shoving snow to the side of the street; that is, whenever they could manage to get out to clear the streets.

The snow continued to fall heavily in large snowflakes. Alan and Dawn were fascinated by the mystical magical white winter wonderland that silently surrounded and engulfed them. The little yellow car struggled, its wheels slipped and the engine roared. Alan rolled down his window, stuck out his arm and reached around to clear off the tiny windshield with his gloved hand. It was becoming hard to see where the street ended and the curb began, but they made the right turn off Mascoutah Avenue onto East Adams. Within a block they faced the real challenge of trying to make the sharp right turn onto George Street and drive up the slight hill there that they thought would surely challenge the little yellow car. They held their breaths while the Volkswagen labored through the ever-deepening snow. But, they did it! They crept up George Street and made the left turn past the apartment building to the back parking area and pulled up near Dawn's apartment back patio door. Alan turned the car off and they sat for a moment and sighed with relief.

"We made it," sighed Dawn, "way to go Alan. You did good."

"I love this little car," Alan said as he patted the dashboard affectionately. Dawn followed suit and patted the dashboard in appreciation.

"I do too," chimed in Dawn, "I love this little car," Dawn let out a big sigh of relief. "It's good to finally be home."

"What a drive that was," sighed Alan.

"Wow, what an adventure," said Dawn so glad to be home and the car parked safely off the street. Dawn patted the dash again, "Thank you," she whispered to the little Volkswagen as if it were a living breathing thing.

"We made it." Alan smiled in relief as he gave Dawn an affectionate hug as they trekked through the snow a couple steps to her back-patio door. Alan felt secure and safe, but he couldn't help but wonder how things were at his house, although he didn't want to say anything to Dawn about his house, so he only expressed concern about his work.

Chapter Seven

Once inside coats, hats, boots removed and wine poured from the big jug, they began to get settled in. Alan knew he needed to call home. He pretended to call work.

"I'm going to have to call work, to see what is going on," Alan lied. Alan was going to call his wife at home and lie to her and tell her that he was stuck at work.

Alan loved the adventure and excitement of living a double life, having his wife and dating Dawn too. He had thought about divorcing Judy, but she was crazy about him and besides she and her father had lots money. Judy's dad paid the down payment on their house and made half of the mortgage payments because it was the biggest house in their Villa Hills subdivision next to Ralph's, and there was no way Alan and Judy could have afforded it on their own. Besides, Judy's dad picked it out and insisted it be theirs.

Alan and Judy had a whorl-wind romance and they got married in a fever. Well, Judy said she was pregnant. It was what her dad called a shotgun wedding, and they needed to get married right away. Neither Alan nor Judy had ever heard the term "shotgun wedding" before; they were just happy that her dad was happy for them and that he was fond of Alan. It was a quickie wedding before a judge that Judy's father knew.

Judy's dad thought that they should have a big wedding but Alan and Judy thought not. Judy's father, an attorney in a large firm with branch offices throughout St. Clair County could easily afford to pay for it. Her dad had said if they weren't going to have a big wedding then he would buy them a house. Alan could feel the painful grip of entrapment in his gut at the time but decided to ignore the feeling.

He wasn't really planning on ever getting married. Alan knew that Ralph Burns, Judy's father, would come after him if he didn't do right and marry his daughter. He was stuck. The family had money; why not get married and enjoy all those nice material things? He just had to accept that his life would be forever changed. Alan did not want to settle down but eventually grew to like the idea of raising a son, or daughter.

And just when he got used to the idea of being a father, tragedy struck. Five weeks after they were married, Judy miscarried and lost the baby while Alan was at work. Judy was devastated, and Alan was hurt and confused. He had just come to accept the fact of becoming a family man, and then things changed.

Alan had a bit of a suspicious mind, and to him Judy did not seem sad and disappointed enough according to Alan's thinking and the way he was feeling. Alan wondered if maybe Judy had not been pregnant after all but really just wanted to get Alan to make up his mind and marry her because he kept putting it off. He wondered if she felt that after dating six months and her dad pressuring her, that they should just get married. Alan wondered, had her father influenced Judy into trapping him into marriage?

Judy's dad had a way of pressuring her into doing things that he wanted her to do. He had reminded her that she was in her thirties, her birth clock was ticking and time was running out, and he dreamed of having a grandson. He told both Judy and Alan as much the first time he had them over for dinner. Alan thought Judy's dad thought that he was a big shot lawyer and could tell Alan what to do and this made Alan leery of him.

Alan had a problem with trusting people as it was because his birth mother gave him up for adoption when he was born. He never knew his birth father and hoped Judy's dad would be a father figure in his life. Now he was not so sure he wanted that because he thought Judy's father, Ralph Burns, big shot lawyer, was overstepping his boundaries.

But maybe Judy had been truthful and indeed pregnant when they got married. After the miscarriage she was on depression medication and slept a lot. Alan was sad that she lost the baby because he actually had gotten use to the idea of being a father, which was immediately cloaked in despair by the reality that Ralph Burns would be in the child's life.

That was four years ago, and Alan wanted out of the marriage now, but he was afraid to ask for a divorce. He was afraid of Ralph Burns. He knew that cheating on Judy was not a good idea, and that her father would probably kill him if he found out. But somehow he got caught up in affairs anyway. Alan's stepfather always cheated on his stepmother, and he merely figured it was a perfectly natural thing to do.

Whenever he thought about asking Judy for a divorce, he would change his mind, because Judy's dad, as if he suspected, would give him that look that said if you hurt my little girl—you're dead. Alan was walking a thin line between feeling imprisoned and cheating to feel free. Sneaking around and secretly dating Dawn made him feel free and gave him a sense of some control to his life.

Chapter Eight

Alan and Dawn were relaxing and watching the local news. They were hoping that the weatherman would say that the snow had ended. But that was not to be the case. Because right then they heard a loud clap of thunder and saw a flash of lightning through the curtains. They jumped up from the couch and stepped out of Dawn's front door to see heavy swirling snowflakes. Huge snowflakes were blowing horizontally. It was exciting in a way to witness such a heavy snowfall of quiet stillness that was spiritually serene and magical. Alan and Dawn were grateful that they had made it safely to Dawn's apartment. Before going inside, they had taken a moment to turn and look around at the silent winter wonderland that surrounded them. Thick snow covered and drooped tree branches, flattened bushes, and was deep on the street and yards. The large amounts of snow looked too heavy for rooftops and it was still snowing and getting deeper and deeper.

"What are you doing?" asked Alan as he followed Dawn as she began to dig in the snow near the front steps? It was obvious to Alan that she was looking for something buried near the shrubbery.

"I am looking for the gallon ofRosé I set out here earlier this evening before we left to go to Greg and Wanda's," laughed Dawn.

"What? Well it should be good and cold."

"Ah, here it is." Dawn found the top of the jug and looped her index finger through the loop in the glass handle and gently pulled it out of the snow.

"Good idea. That's what I like about you, you are always thinking." He hoped too that Dawn bought a lot of groceries because he knew, that the way the snow was coming down, he wasn't going anywhere anytime soon. They barely made to her place, so he knew he wasn't going anywhere until after the snowplows came through, and he knew they would wait until the snowfall ended before they would even attempt to plow any roads.

"Pour me a glass ofRosé will you," Dawn asked as she placed the full jug on the counter. Dawn was glad she had bought a big gallon ofRosé while she was at the store several days earlier. She was intuitive and her intuition had made her wonder if the weatherman had the correct forecast even back then. Within the last hour the forecast was once again updated predicting several more days of snowfall.

Dawn wasn't too crazy about all the snow that would entrap them, but she did look forward to the idea that she and Alan would be together, and she would have him all to herself. Oh, he had spent the night before, many times, but several days in a row would be a new experience. Alan would be all hers, stuck at her place as advised by the weatherman and Illinois Department of Transportation.

"Sure thing, Babe," Alan said as he got two wine glasses from the kitchen cupboard. Dawn reached up and kissed him on the lips as she passed him on her way to the bedroom to change into her comfy sweats.

It was time for wine and Alan poured himself a glass too. He was thinking the same thing as Dawn. He was stuck there, and he wondered if he could handle three days of sexual bliss and constant togetherness. When Dawn closed the bedroom door, Alan called out to her from the kitchen announcing that he was making a phone call.

"Hey Babe, I received a page and I am going to call work and see how things are going there," announced Alan. He thought if he told Dawn that he was going to be on the phone, that it would keep her from calling out to him, asking hm what he wanted when she heard his voice while he was on the phone talking to his wife. He certainly did not want Judy to hear Dawn's voice in the background as he was talking to her on the phone. Yeah, he said that he was going to call work, but that was a lie, he called his wife at home instead.

Chapter Nine

"Hey Babe, how you doing?" he asked his wife when she answered the phone.

"I was worried about you," Judy said. She sounded tired.

"You doing okay?" Alan asked her. "You sound sleepy." She slept a lot lately. Alan knew it was the Valium that she took for anxiety. He figured she was hooked on them. She had begun taking them soon after the miscarriage claiming to feel depressed. She drank a lot of wine too, and he hoped it would not interfere with the Valium and cause serious side effects.

"Yes, I was just dozing off," she announced. She was bored. Judy was bored with her father overseeing everything she did, and she was bored with Alan who worked all the time, or so it seemed. And now she was bored with all the snow that had fallen and had her trapped at home.

She had called her managers in her three hair styling salons, and of course they all stayed home as all their clients had cancelled due to the horrific snowfall. The national weather bureau and all the news stations on the radio and television broadcasted warnings not to go out but to stay home and off the roads that due to the blizzard conditions and large amount of snowfall the St. Louis Metropolitan area. The Transportation Department in both Missouri and Illinois had ordered everyone to stay home so the roads could eventually be cleared when the snow fall ended.

"How are you?" Judy asked. "It's getting very bad out on the streets dad said." She had just talked with him. He had advised her to stay home and not go out.

Judy's dad lived right down the street and checked in often, either by calling or walking over to see if Judy was home and what she was up to. Since her mother died years earlier, her dad was even more into her life. Judy couldn't make a move without her dad stepping in to either help or offer advice. Between Alan and her dad, Judy was felt very trapped. She was happy she had her job so she could be her own boss at work, if no place else.

She was proud of her successful businesses. She owned and operated three hair salons in the Belleville area. She enjoyed the options of managing and taking a few appointments which she did part-time. Styling part-time kept her in practice and up to date with the latest techniques, styles, and hair products. She also liked the fact that if she did not feel like going to the salons she could manage them from home. Her salon hairstylist knew that she was only a phone call away if something came up and they had to consult her. Judy's business was very profitable. Her stylists rented their styling stations from her but ordered their own supplies, leaving less responsibility for Judy. She enjoyed her job and the people she worked with.

"Yes, it's getting deep all right, I need to stay here at work," said Alan trying to sound disappointed, "no one can come in because of the road conditions. So I may have to stay put for a couple of days."

The tale he told was good he thought. Judy knew the electricians at Monsanto had a well-supplied kitchen and well stocked freezer and refrigerator. Most of the guys were game hunters and fisherman who would bring in their kill and catch and cook it up for the six electricians that worked there around the clock. The guys had to be there in case there was a problem, so there was a lot of down time while they waited for dispatch to call them. When they weren't working, they usually spent their time cooking.

Alan hung up the phone just as Dawn opened the bedroom door. Alan was off the hook, or so he thought. Little did he know that earlier that day Judy called Alan at work and a co-worker who answered the call looked for Alan and said he was not there, but that he could be in another building. "I'll have him call you when I see him," the co-worker said. Alan's co-worker knew Alan well enough to realize he needed to be vague when his wife called, and Alan was not at work.

Judy's dad had his own way of thinking about Alan. Being a prosecuting attorney for many years made him suspicious of any man in his daughter's life. When he called Judy and she said that Alan was not at home but at work, he questioned her.

"You said the guy who answered the phone at Alan's work said he was not there?" asked Ralph.

"That is what I am saying," said Judy, "but Alan just called and said he was at work and would probably have to cover all the shifts for a couple of days. No one else can come in because of orders to stay off the roadways,"

"Well, it sounds suspicious to me," said Ralph, "I'll see what I can find out."

Alan was naïve thinking that he was actually getting away with something. He had no idea that Judy's father was suspicious of him. Alan actually enjoyed this cat and mouse game he played thinking he was fooling his wife, her dad, and Dawn. He liked being daring and seeing what he could get away with, without getting caught. Sneaking around made life more exciting.

Chapter Ten

"Is everything okay?" Dawn asked. She was all cozy and comfy since she had changed into warm fleece sweats and slipped into her slippers. Alan always kept a bag of clothes in his car so he was prepared and got comfortable too. They snuggled up and settled in to watch the late news on television. The weatherman repeatedly suggested everyone stay off the roads so snowplows could get out and clear the streets after the snow stopped. Only problem was, the snow was expected to continue at least through Sunday, including Monday and maybe even into Tuesday. Up to twenty-two inches of snow was expected and the temperatures were predicted to stay below freezing, so it wasn't going to melt anytime soon.

"Twenty-two inches of snow," Dawn said as she refilled Alan's wine glass, "can you believe it." Yes, a roommate, Dawn thought. She thought that it was going to be fun having Alan trapped there in her little love nest for a while. It made her heart stir thinking of all the sexual intimacy they would share.

"Yep supervisor at work said to stay off the roads," stated Alan sounding very convincing he thought.

"Gosh, who would have thought it would snow this much?" Dawn said with a grin.

"Looks like I'm yours for a least three days and a gallon ofRosé," he kissed her and then they clinked their wine glasses together and made a toast to the blizzard.

"Three days and a gallon ofRosé," giggled Dawn, "I can handle that."

"Oh, maybe I should drink sparingly," smiled Alan bringing the glass to his lips to take a sip.

"Oh, I have another gallon in the pantry, just in case," laughed Dawn. They clinked glasses and each took a sip.

"We better call Greg and Wands before it gets too late, they'll be wanting to know if we made it home okay," Alan suggested. He really wanted to lead Dawn into the bedroom but knew they better call first.

Greg and Wanda were thrilled to hear from them. "We were just about to call you," warned Wanda, "we were worried about you."

Alan and Dawn gave them a full report of the road conditions. They told them that they did not see a single snowplow on the roads. Nothing was touched and it was getting very deep.

"It's so deep" reported Alan, "I don't know where they would shove all the snow. And any cars parked on the streets will be buried for a long time." No one was driving anywhere for a while.

"Yes, its deep over here and no snowplows in sight," reported Wanda. "Well, we are glad that you made it home safely. We surely enjoyed your company," said Wanda. She loved to flirt with Alan. Alan was a handsome guy, tall dark, good physique and looked great sporting the start of a beard.

Alan and Dawn settled on the living room couch after talking to Greg and Wanda. He wanted to hear the local weather report. Alan was watching the television sipping wine and smoking a Swisher Sweet cigar, when the phone rang.

"I'll get it," announced Dawn as she got up from the couch and picked up the wall phone in the kitchen.

"Hello," Dawn said as she picked up the receiver hoping it was Nancy who was calling, and it was. Dawn's heart jumped when she heard Nancy's voice. Funny, she thought, when Alan called her heart never jumped quite like that. Dawn chalked it up to desire for forbidden fruit, wanting something she knew was out of reach or maybe wanting it simply because she knew she couldn't have it and it was safe to dream about it.

Dawn hated to admit to herself that she had a crush on Nancy. No one in their right mind wants to be gay she thought to herself. She could not bring herself to even say the word "lesbian," so she kept her feelings for Nancy to herself. It was her little secret, no one knew, not even Nancy, certainly not Alan.

But Dawn was always extra excited when they got to double date with Nancy and Gerry or when Nancy invited her to go to the bar, or go shopping or ride with her to visit her aunt and uncle who lived in Waterloo. Nancy took her breath away. Whatever Nancy wanted to do was fine with Dawn, just as long as she could spend time with her.

Nancy was strong-willed and had a great sense of humor, lots of common sense, was smart as a whip. She was advancing professionally as a manager at the Ralston Purina Company in St. Louis. She managed her life well, and Dawn was in awe of her. They both dated guys so it went without saying, of course, they were not lesbians. And even if Dawn thought that Nancy might have hinted at it from time to time—there was no way that Dawn was making the move and taking a chance of losing her best friend or of being ostracized from their group of friends.

Dawn was not a lesbian—or so she kept telling herself. She did not think that she fit the profile. Besides she was dating Alan, and he made her feel, well normal. She felt it certainly was a mixed up, shook up world with a lot of differences in human nature.

"How are you doing?" Nancy wanted to know, and she sounded concerned. Dawn could tell that Nancy was puffing on a cigarette, probably a Tareyton 100. Dawn smoked the same brand of cigarettes when she was out drinking. They both "would rather fight than switch" as the Tareyton 100 magazine advertisements would picture a girl with one black eye. She heard Nancy take a puff and it made Dawn want to light one up too, so she stretched and extended the wall phone cord to the max until she could reach her open purse sitting on a kitchen chair. With her free hand she reached in and pulled out her cigarette case and lighter. She managed to open a fresh pack, tap it on her left hand until a cigarette poked out and lit it up, inhaled and exhaled. She could hear Nancy exhale then too and smiled. It seemed Dawn smoked the most cigarettes while on the phone talking to Nancy, or really whenever she was with Nancy.

"Oh, we just got home from Greg and Wanda's," reported Dawn as she took a drag from her cigarette and gave Nancy a complete report of the evening's events and road conditions.

"Gerry is here," announced Nancy, "we stayed in. It looks like we will be staying put for a while. I hate that I will miss work, I have so much going on there right now, and I would like to get to it."

Nancy was an enthusiastic manager looking to climb the ladder at Ralston Purina.

Gerry was not as ambitious as Nancy. He preferred a more casual work environment and liked his non-stressful job at an auto parts supply store. She was the serious one in the relationship, and Gerry was more of a jokester, relaxed and worry free. But, no matter their personality differences, somehow their relationship seemed to work for them. They had met at Tim and Joe's bar and restaurant and had been dating for several months; which for Nancy was a long time to date the same guy.

They both had orders from their employers to stay home and not to try to come to work. Businesses were honoring Illinois and Missouri Departments of Transportation request for drivers to stay off the roadways so clearing equipment could get out there when the snow stopped to get the roadways cleared.

"Just wanted to make sure you were okay," said Nancy sounding concerned.

"We are fine," smiled Dawn, hearing Nancy's concern warmed her heart. "Glad to hear you and Gerry are okay too."

"Hey next weekend if you are not busy and the roads are okay by then, do you want to ride down to Waterloo with me to visit my aunt and uncle, Gerry will be working," Nancy was missing Dawn, and Dawn could hear it in her voice.

"Sure, sounds good," Dawn replied eager to spend the day, just the two of them, hanging out together without the fellas. Dawn missed Nancy too, at times she hated playing second fiddle to Gerry, but that was just the way it was. Dawn knew that she would never be number one in Nancy's life.

"I haven't seen my aunt and uncle for a while," Nancy said then added. "They said they'll have lunch for us." Nancy liked to visit her aunt and uncle; they were a lot of fun. Nancy's younger sister still lived with them. Her two brothers were older and had already moved out and were on their own. Her aunt and uncle had taken in all the kids several years back when their parents were killed in an auto accident. The sad tragic story of Nancy losing both parents in an accident found a soft spot in Dawn's heart and she was glad to set aside any Saturday chores in order to join Nancy and spend time with her.

Chapter Eleven

It was Sunday morning and still snowing when Dawn woke up and peeked out from behind the curtains to see what the morning had brought in the way of snowfall. There was even more snow that covered up their footprints from the night before.

"What a night," said Dawn, "did you sleep well?"

"Yes, sure did without the sounds of traffic, it was very quiet, except for your snoring," Alan laughed as he leaned over and gave Dawn a kiss as she slipped back under the covers.

"You must have been hearing yourself," she quirked back, "because I do not snore." She kissed him back and their kisses turned to love making. Dawn loved making love with Alan. He was very gentle, attentive, sweet and loving. But after the loving when he laid with his arm around her, Dawn felt that something was missing.

There was a void in her heart that he just could not fill. She thought of Nancy during those times and wondered could Nancy fill that void. Dawn was good at making excuses for what she could not have. She actually thought that her and Nancy's personalities would probably clash if they actually were together.

She couldn't see them living together and getting along well; besides society would frown.

Who was she kidding; Dawn couldn't see herself living with Alan either. She was a confused mess and she knew it but thought she hid it well. It was why Dawn preferred a casual, carefree social life of hanging out with the group just having fun going to parties, to the bar for dancing, and casual care-free conversation. Nothing serious was her motto.

Chapter Twelve

After lunch Alan and Dawn decided to take a walk up Mascoutah Avenue toward East Main Street just to see what was going on and to see just how deep the snow was getting. Cabin fever was setting in already, so it was great to get outdoors and play in the snow. They planned on walking in the middle of the street. There were no vehicles to get in the way, or make noise, or spew exhaust or make dirty tracks in the beautiful snow.

The snow, which was pristine and beautiful, covered everything with a sparkling white thick blanket of insulation that made all the outdoors very peaceful and beautiful. It was so quiet it made Dawn and Alan feel like they should whisper as to not disturb the serenity of it. The snow was wonderful to walk in even though her boots were not quite high enough to keep her pant legs from getting wet up to her knees.

She took big steps to try to walk in Alan's footsteps. They laughed as Alan tried to take smaller steps in order for her to walk in his footsteps. He slipped and nearly fell and they both broke into laugher. Occasionally, they met fellow trekkers also walking down the middle of the street and greeted them with big smiles and comments about how beautiful everything was. There was something about this beautiful surprise blizzard that put everyone in a happy mood. Everyone was joyful and very friendly and filled with awe of the beautiful wonder of nature. They were forced to stay off the roads and be home and so they loved the mandatory break from their normal everyday routines.

Dawn loved that the heavy snowfall seemed to have lifted the spirits of everyone. It felt magical because everyone was so happy as if a certain electricity was left in the air after the all the lightning that occurred during the snowstorm. It was as if the area needed a mystical magical break from the ordinary routines of life. The break was truly a gift from nature that filled the air with happiness as people were ordered not to go to school, or work, and not to drive anywhere. So people just wanted to get out in it and play.

"I wonder if anything is open," asked Alan rather breathless from trekking through deep snow as he looked up the street at the store fronts.

"It's hard telling," answered Dawn, "maybe just the bars and restaurants where proprietors live in the same building or close by."

"I just saw someone go into that corner tavern up the street called Lill's," announced Alan looking ahead about a block up the street. Dawn was too busy watching where she was walking and trying to stay in Alan's tracks to notice where he was looking.

Suddenly she felt a sense of nervous excitement and

anticipation. She had always wanted to go into that bar, but was always too afraid to venture in alone. And her friends never talked about going there and she never wanted to bring it up and make a suggestion. Lill's tavern was a lesbian bar or so she had heard.

Dawn had a special place in her heart for women. It was obvious to her, since she had a secret crush on Nancy. But she knew she could not be a lesbian for real, because the women that went to Lill's tavern were not like her. Oh, she didn't fancy herself as being highly feminine, but she dated men, right? Men must have seen something feminine in her; they asked her out, didn't they? So she couldn't be a lesbian.

When they got closer to Lil's they could see that the bar was open. They looked at each other in a what-do-you-think way.

"Want to give it a try?" asked Alan. Dawn had told him she thought that it was a women's bar. He didn't flinch at the possibility being the only guy in a bar full of women; but rather appeared intrigued if maybe a little nervous like she was.

"Sure, why not," Dawn replied feeling a little anxious. Dawn had recently seen a couple of lesbians holding hands while sitting at the bar at Panorama Lounge. The two women appeared to be arguing over something but only for a few minutes, then they kissed and hugged and made up, right there in front of everyone at the bar, and no one said or did anything.

Which was rather curious to Dawn, because one night at Tim and Joe's two women sat at the bar and starting kissing. Tim was tending bar at the time and saw them kissing, and asked them to leave, which they did. So, Dawn really had mixed feelings about all this gay stuff. In a way, she was jealous, because apparently those women knew where they fit in society, and she did not. They appeared happy to be who they were.

It actually depressed Dawn because in her heart she wondered just where did she really fit in. She didn't think that she was like any of the women at the two bars incidences that she witnessed. At least they had it figured out where they belonged. Here she was a supposedly straight woman having crushes on straight women. When Dawn was driving to work one day, she had heard a popular radio psychologist calm a worried mother by saying that all young girls have crushes on other girls while growing up. She reassured the mother by telling her that by the time girls become young women they would have grown out of those girl crushes. Hearing that made Dawn's heart sink because it was not very reassuring. She had not grown out of her girl crushes. That radio show message haunted her.

She felt better when she listened to a radio show another morning while driving to work. She heard a different host named Dr. Joy Browne, and Dawn heard another opinion that made her feel better. A woman had called the psychologist saying her daughter came out to her as a lesbian. The mother was distraught because she did not want her daughter to be a lesbian. It felt disgraceful to her, and she was worried about what would people think. The woman sounded like she was only concerned about her own standing in the community; that, a daughter loving someone of the same sex, and going against the grain of society, would be an embarrassment to her and make it difficult for her to face her friends. The woman sounded selfish to Dawn and evidently sounded selfish to the psychologist too.

"Do you want your daughter to be happy?" asked the psychologist.

"Well, yes, but adult life is not always happy," said the mother. It made Dawn wonder if the mother was a lesbian herself but pretended to be straight and married a man to keep her parents happy and to fit religious and social norms. Dawn thought the mother sounded as if she thought that her daughter should suffer right along with the other straight mothers who perhaps had unhappy marriages, or maybe were latent lesbian themselves. But as it was, religion and society shamed women and men and corralled them into distinct categories of what religion and society dictated as normal. Dawn felt a sudden pang of hope and joy as the soft-hearted psychologist responded to the mother's concerns.

"What is more important, your thoughts of social norms or your daughter's happiness?" asked Dr. Browne. From the way the mother talked, it was apparent that the daughter had no qualms as to what people thought of her relationship with another woman. She was happy in her relationship. It was the mother who was put out.

"Love is love, and if two people are happily in love,

then what is more important than that?" added the psychologist. There was dead silence after that, so it was apparent that the mother on the phone was speechless. The woman had no argument; she could not argue that she did not want her daughter to be happy.

Chapter Thirteen

Dawn and Alan stood on the somewhat snow cleared steps of the lesbian bar holding hands, smiling and looking into each other's eyes for a sign of courage. He nodded, as she stepped inside while he held the door open for her. She took three brave steps as he followed close behind as they entered the bar. Alan and Dawn looked around in wonder as they stood inside the door and waited for their eyes to adjust to the low light of the room. It was quiet as if all the women had all stopped talking to one another to look at the two clueless straight people who wandered in. It was so dim that Alan and Dawn could barely make out the staring figures in the darkened bar, but they knew they were being stared at. Dawn felt very conspicuous. Alan stood next to a bar as close to the door as he could possibly be. He gently pulled Dawn towards the stool to sit next to him. Dawn was nervous and sensed that Alan was uneasy. Their eyes had finally adjusted, and they could make out the women at the pool table and down at the other end of the bar who slowly got back to their conversations and their pool game.

The large bosom barmaid slowly strolled over their

way without a smile. Dawn didn't think she was very friendly, as she did not say a word or make an effort to smile a welcoming smile for Dawn and Alan. She finally stopped and stood directly in front of Dawn giving Dawn a wink and a slight smile, which did not go, unnoticed by Alan. Alan had no idea why he felt more left out and ignored rather than jealous. When the barmaid finally got finished flirting with Dawn, she asked her what she wanted to drink.

"I'll have a glass of beer," Dawn said rather shyly.

"We will have two glasses of whatever is on draft," interjected Alan suddenly pointing at the beer tap near where the barmaid stood. Alan's jest broke the spell between the barmaid and a shy Dawn who had not been able to break away from the intense stare of the clear greeneyed barmaid.

Alan had sounded rather shy himself when he ordered the beers, which even surprised Dawn. The barmaid looked Alan and Dawn up and down and wanted to giggle because she couldn't decide if the straight couple was snow struck or lesbian struck, as if they had never seen this much snow before or this many lesbians before. She only smiled.

"I got Stag on draft," she offered in a rather business like take-it-or-leave-it tone.

"We will each have a glass of Stag," said Alan after making eye contact with Dawn. He tried to appear more comfortable in an uncomfortable situation by leaning close to Dawn and resting his elbow on the bar as he propped his foot on the boot rail. He would try to steady himself throughout the duration of this unexpected and frankly new experience. He had never been into a gay bar. Oh, he had heard lots of talk of people going over to a gay bar called Faces in East St. Louis, after all the bars closed in Belleville and St Louis, but he had never ventured there himself.

Dawn turned on her bar stool slightly in order to get a better look at the huge mirror behind the bar. It was beautiful oak trimmed in dark stain and practically covered the whole wall. The building was old with lots of ornately carved decorative oak wood on all the walls. There was wide dark stained wood trim around the big double windows that faced the street. And it had the old-style metal ornate ceiling that so many old buildings had.

She had to admit that the place, clients and atmosphere was interesting enough, but Dawn looked out the window to the street and wished she was out there rather than sitting at the bar feeling strange as if she had ventured out into the infinite abyss of blanketed snow and somehow landed on another planet. She had a Star Wars colorful characters bar scene moment as if the world had suddenly changed totally with the beautifully serene setting outdoors and the colorful collection of characters the bar scene inside.

She could hear the women talking and laughing at someone's joke. Someone dropped coins into the jukebox and Olivia Newton-John could be heard singing," Please Mister Please, don't play B17." Soon some of the women were singing along. Dawn stole a glance in the mirror behind the bar and her eyes met one of the women's stares as she mouthed "it was my song, it was her song," swaying to the music she winked at Dawn as she danced a slow dance by herself.

Dawn jumped in a startled reaction then just as the very noticeable busty barmaid-tending bar returned with two glasses of beer leaned slightly over in front of Dawn, hesitating a bit. Dawn couldn't help but stare at her huge breast with lots of cleavage that showed from the woman's unbuttoned blouse. It was hard to break her stare, but Dawn managed and cast her eyes down and stared at the beer in front of her. The barmaid smiled and slowly strolled away.

Alan took a sip then leaned closer and whispered in Dawn's ear. He had been watching the women at the other end of the bar and the one staring at Dawn.

"I think that one dancing in front of the jukebox likes you," he said with an amused tone to his voice.

"Very funny," Dawn whispered back without looking at him but rather staring into her glass of beer before taking a much-needed slug of the cold and refreshing brew that slightly burned on the way down.

The glass of Stag beer was cold and bitter which Dawn thought was so very fitting for the heavily cliquish atmosphere of the bar. Stag beer was popular in Belleville mostly because it was brewed in Belleville. Stag beer had been brewed there since the 1850s. The brewery employed a couple hundred dedicated family linage employees. Dawn's friend Gene worked there, as did his dad and grandfather before him. Stag beer brewery had been a proud family tradition for generations. Gene often talked of working shift work. He would work the midnight shift and get off work at eight in the morning. It was customary when a worker got off work in the morning to stop in the nearby tavern to have bacon and eggs and a glass of Stag beer for breakfast.

"You drink beer at eight o'clock in the morning?" Dawn asked Gene. He would only smile in response, so she never knew if he was joking or not about having beer with breakfast. But just as his father, and grandfather before him, as a loyal and faithful employees, he only drank Stag beer.

Alan and Dawn chatted amongst themselves amid the curious occasional looks of the clientele who all appeared to be regulars at the establishment. Feeling more than a little out of place, Alan and Dawn quickly drank their glasses of beer, got up, nodded good-bye to the barmaid and waved to the room of cat-like stares of the women as they made their way out the door into the cold.

The frigid air felt refreshing on their faces as they breathed it in. It felt good to get outside where the air was pristine, clear, quiet, and serene. Out in nature, where everything made sense and had the feeling of normalcy—it snowed in winter, flowers bloomed in springtime and animals paired off, mated, built nests and had little ones. Everything so predictable and easily understood.

They walked toward Dawn's apartment in silence

mostly, each in their own thoughts. They only talked a bit about how they enjoyed the natural simplicity of nature as both took in its wonders in all its glory easily explained and sane and such a distinct contrast to the complexity of human nature.

They trekked down the middle of the street making many more footprints in the snow that would one day melt away, unlike the memories of their first gay bar experience which would be etched in their minds for a long time. As they walked along, each one was thinking how the experience of being together, feeling the electricity that charged the air was somehow changing them. There certainly was something in the air all right; something was brought out in each of them and would only rise to the surface within each in their own due time.

The day felt refreshingly magical somehow to both in their own way. They felt somehow lighter and freer not knowing why, at the moment, only time would tell for each of them. As if coming back to reality, they began to talk about their Lill's experience. They both agreed Lill's place was very interesting and a step into another world, one in which they both had to admit they found intriguing and a little scary. They decided it was scary only because they were not familiar with that type of lifestyle or with Stag beer, for that matter, and they both had to laugh.

Without words, when they got back to Dawn's they hurriedly pulled off their boots and undressed each other on the way to the bedroom. Why were they so aroused? Without sharing their thoughts, they both wondered if they were trying to convince the other or themselves that they were really straight? Or were they both aroused somehow by the gay experience and were eager to have sex, looking forward to silently enjoying their own secret same sex fantasies as they made love.

Chapter Fourteen

It was fun for Dawn to have Alan there with her all the time. But she realized that just as unpredictable as the blizzard was, that one day as sure as the snow would melt their hot lovemaking would cool down too. She realized temporary extreme weather conditions such as a novelty record-breaking snowfall helped to keep their relationship interesting. It was as if the static electricity of the thunder and lightning that brought the many inches of thunder snow lingered in the air to create an excitingly super charged atmospheric pressure change to the area.

And like the weather outdoors the atmosphere in Dawn's apartment was electric and exciting. But one can only have so much sex, drink so much wine, and watch just so many HBO cable movies before even that becomes humdrum. Her one bedroom, one bathroom apartment really was without much personal privacy. Having always lived alone, Dawn was actually surprised that she did not mind sharing her small space. She enjoyed Alan's company and hoped he enjoyed hers, but she could see that he was getting restless and anxious. She knew that he wondered how things were at his apartment. He smiled when the local newsman said the plows were preparing to get out and about and it wouldn't be long before people could return to their normal routines. What was normal anyway? As far as Alan and Dawn's personal lives were concerned, both were somehow changed.

Alan said he had received a page from work, as he and Dawn had just finished watching "ET" The Extra-Terrestrial movie and were discussing the possibility of the reality of alien life. Dawn believed in aliens, but Alan said he needed more convincing evidence.

"I need to call work," Alan said in a low voice as he got up to walk to the kitchen wall phone to make a phone call. Dawn figured it was in regard to his upcoming work schedule. She figured people living out in the country probably wouldn't make it in to work for several more days. Her boss had just called her and told her to come in on Wednesday. Alan had listened to her phone call and now he wanted to call work.

Alan spoke very low when he got on the phone, which puzzled Dawn. She wondered why he was being secretive. He had listened to her phone call why did he speak just above a whisper and stretch the phone cord to its full extent so it would reach into the bathroom, where he stood with his back to the door to talk. Dawn thought it was rather curious and tried to listen from the kitchen where she began preparing a big bowl of salad, to go with the spaghetti she was preparing to have for dinner. As hard as she tried, she could just barely hear Alan's voice and could not make out what he was saying. It left her feeling rather curious.

Chapter Fifteen

Judy, I don't know how long it will be," Alan tried not to sound aggravated, "I have to stay here at work until I can be relieved."

"How do I know you are really at work?" snapped Judy.

"What?" Alan couldn't believe she was questioning him.

"Dad said he called your work and they couldn't find you, just like when I tried to call you yesterday evening."

"What?" Alan raised his voice, but then remembered to lower it again so Dawn would not hear him. Why the hell was Judy's dad calling his workplace? The audacity he thought, and that made him furious. The man should mind his own business, Alan thought.

"Well, when that man at your work couldn't find you, I got worried," complained Judy. "So when I told Dad that I was worried about you, he tried to call you too."

"You do know that I work in several buildings. I go from building to building, wherever I am needed to fix problems," Alan was suddenly angered, but he couldn't let on and he had to keep quiet so Dawn wouldn't hear.

"I get that," said Judy, "but still I thought someone would know where you were." She was beginning to sound less irritated and even a little more understanding, and Alan was relieved to hear it.

I'm a roving technician, for god's sake, Alan thought. He hated explaining his every move, and now Judy's dad was sticking his nose into his business and whereabouts.

"What was that's guy's name," asked Alan trying to cover his tracks. "It was probably one of the guys that is on loan around here and doesn't know who is who yet."

"I don't know what his name is, but he sounded like he knew you. He kind of snickered though when I asked where you were. But he just said that you were not in the building. He said he was a rover and was in and out and he just got a work page and had to go. He made me feel like I was bothering him."

"Well, he was probably busy and in the middle of working on something," said Alan wanting to tell her that on a snowy weekend you can expect there would be all kinds of problems with the equipment at work, but he just let it go.

"Well, okay, that makes sense," Judy was backing down. She always got like this when she was home alone. Alan always told her that she needed more hobbies and projects to keep her busy. She just thought too much, and her imagination grew wild. Alan told her

she should be a writer. Write a book he would tell her.
She needed to put her imagination to paper. Even her
dad told her she wasn't happy unless she was worrying
about something.

Chapter Sixteen

Judy was worried; she decided she did not believe Alan was at work. She called her dad as she always did whenever she worried about anything that Alan was doing.

"You know Judy, I think maybe you do worry too much," Ralph said. He was concerned too about his daughter and the man she married but at the moment wanted to calm her down a bit.

"Well, something does not seem right," insisted Judy almost in tears.

"How about I come over and we'll talk a bit," suggested Ralph knowing all too well that his suspicions made her suspicious too. Alan was nice enough, but Ralph had his concerns. Ralph liked living close by and walked over to Judy's house almost every day. He trekked through the deep snow to check on her, but today he wanted to drive the truck to see her after he cleared the driveway a bit.

Ralph liked to keep busy. He couldn't get to his office so made all his phone calls to clients from his home office. Having finished his phone calls, he walked out into the garage and grabbed the snow shovel and was going to shovel the driveway. He got the shock of his life when he opened the garage door and faced a wall of snow.

"Holy shit," He declared. There was at least four feet of snowdrifts facing him. He took his snow shovel and poked at it a bit not making much of a dent. In no time at all, he worked up a sweat and could feel his face getting red as his heart was racing. He took a break remembering the warnings on television news about how too much shoveling could cause a heart attack.

"Oh, the hell with it," he complained out loud to himself and threw the snow shovel in the corner and climbed into his truck. Ralph had a big four-wheel drive pick-up truck equipped with a new snowplow blade mounted on the front. He had had the foresight and good sense to back his truck into the garage so all he had to do was drive forward to get out.

He knew his truck could easily maneuver through the deep snow as It sat high. He was eager to try it and get out and play in the snow. He wanted to see where he could drive it and how much snow he could clear. As he sat behind the wheel of his truck and looked out of his garage he could barely see above the snow drifts. In the distance Ralph could see a guy in a big high-profile four-wheeler truck plow through the snow and he seemed to make it okay. It appeared that some snowplows had been out already in the neighborhood.

He thought about driving to work but quickly changed his mind. No sense in trying to drive to the office because neither partners nor clients could make it in with the roads covered with snow. He decided to drive over to Judy's house. Ralph gunned the engine, dropped the blade and plowed through the snowdrifts to get out of his garage. He was amazed by all the snow that covered the area. As it was, he could barely clear just enough room by carefully shoving and pushing snow to the side enough to drive out to the street. The big four-wheel pick-up struggled, but he made it over to Judy's driveway and lowered the snow blade and cleared her driveway too as she watched from the front window. He worked for nearly an hour until she signaled for him to come inside for a cup of coffee.

"There sits my little worry wart." Ralph smiled as he came in the house and saw her sitting at the kitchen table drinking fresh brewed coffee.

"Well, I don't think that I worry too much," Judy told her dad.

Ralph stood at the counter with his back to her and poured himself a cup of coffee. He carefully pulled out his flask from his vest pocket where she could not see it then poured a little Irish whiskey in his cup of coffee.

"Oh, you know you do," he said as he stirred his coffee. He couldn't resist kidding her. He put the teaspoon down and slowly turned with his cup and sat down across from her at the table.

"Oh Dad, now you know very well, that Alan could have slipped and fallen on the ice somewhere at work. And who knows when they would have found him," Judy stubbornly pointed out.

"It's a big place, I'm sure, there are lots of people

walking around there all the time, don't you think?" reasoned her dad feeling confident he knew what he was talking about.

"There's something else, Dad," Judy said. Her dad heard a familiar tone to her voice that sounded like her mother when she used to get so worried about things. He loved his daughter dearly, but she was so sensitive. He knew he spoiled and pampered her after her mother died years ago, but she was his little girl and always would be.

"What is it, baby?" He knew something was really bothering her and he sat up straight and listened closely.

"Oh, Dad," Judy was practically in tears.

"What is going on—are you ill?" wondered Ralph. "Tell me," he demanded. He was worried. He did not want her to get sick and die like her mother did.

"No, I am not ill," smirked Judy as if it would almost be easier to deal with an illness.

"Then what is it?" he demanded.

"I think something is going on with Alan."

"What?" asked Ralph, "Is he sick?" He tried to sound more concerned than irritated. He didn't know if he was more annoyed at Alan or Judy, or both of them. Lately, they seemed to be very mismatched. Alan was outgoing and friendly, and Judy was an introvert and moody like her mother was. Ralph always felt his wife Susan's emotions were way out of sync with reality. She was never happy. Ralph thought that her emotions caught up with her and eventually gave her cancer.

"What, for god's sake?" snorted Ralph getting himself

a second cup of coffee. While keeping his back turned to her, he again secretly spiked it with a generous shot of Irish whiskey. He was glad that he had filled his flask to the top before he left home; apparently it was going to be a long visit.

"Whatever it is, I'll take care of it. Nobody hurts my baby girl." He smiled, the booze beginning to take its hold.

"You will?" asked Judy.

"Of course, haven't I always," he claimed. He was sincere then, and he knew Judy could hear it in his voice. He was halfway serious and halfway making light of what was on her mind. Judy had always been very emotional and very sensitive. He spoiled her and he knew it. Judy was an only child and so they dotted on her. Judy was all that Ralph had now that his wife was gone. Susan had lost her long battle with cancer and it was hard on him but even more difficult on Judy losing her mother. Her mother was her best friend. Ralph listened patiently as Judy continued.

"I'm afraid Alan is having an affair," Judy said with a shaky voice and tears in her eyes.

"What makes you think that Alan is having an affair?" Ralph asked thinking how dare he.

"I'll kill him," Ralph shouted, and then realized he spoke out loud. As soon as he said it, he wished he could take it back. He knew it was the whiskey talking. He got up went over to the coffee pot and topped off his cup with coffee leaving enough room for the whiskey he felt he desperately needed. He was sure she did not see him since her head was lowered as she sat staring into her cup of coffee. He quietly sat down at the table across from her and leaned forward resting his elbows on the table.

"I smelled some woman's perfume that was not mine on his shirt, when I was gathering clothes to do laundry," Judy was becoming emotional now.

"That's it?" Ralph wanted to know. He knew he sounded sarcastic. "Oh, well that's hardly evidence enough." Ralph knew he sounded like an attorney in Alan's defense. Probably the wrong thing to do as he knew it would only further upset her, so he backed off.

"Well, it was enough for me," cried Judy, "so I followed him last Wednesday."

"You did what?" Ralph couldn't believe what he was hearing.

"When I called him at work, he told me he had to work overtime," Judy said becoming rather emotional. "I know he gets off at eleven, so I drove pass a couple of the bars I figured he always went to." Judy hesitated a moment to wipe her tears then blow her nose then she continued.

"I finally found his car at one of the bars," she said through tears.

"Where did you find him?" Ralph was curious now and sat up straight in his chair, leaning forward so he could listen more intently and not miss a word.

"When I drove around the back-parking lot of Panorama Lounge, I saw his car."

"Well, if he was going for a drink after work, he should have told you that and not lied," Ralph came to her defense.

"Well, Dad, that is exactly what I thought," cried Judy reaching for another tissue.

"So, did you go home then, after you saw his car," asked Ralph feeling much like a protective father now.

"Well, I was going too, but then when I was about to leave the parking lot, I saw him come out of the door. He was walking out with a girl." Judy had to blow her nose again and wipe her eyes before she continued.

"What happened then?" Ralph wanted to know. He was becoming impatient and anxious and wanted to learn more.

"He walked her to her car. Then walked over to his car and got in. I thought that was harmless enough. I sat in my car and continued to watch and then I saw him head in the opposite direction of home and in the same direction that she was headed."

"So he did not head in the direction of home." Ralph wanted to be sure he was hearing her correctly, so he made her repeat it. For a moment he felt that he was back in the courtroom cross-examining a witness and repeating the statement so the court reporter could confirm it and record the information a second time.

"Alan drove like he knew where he was going, because he did not act like he was trying to keep up with her in order to follow her. He knew where he was going," Dawn said through tears.

"I see, go on," Ralph was becoming even more

concerned now. He was up out of the chair and pacing now, as if in a court room, continuing with his questioning of the witness.

"I followed him to her apartment," Judy said with the tone of growing anger in her voice." I had to be careful because she lives on a dead-end street and I did not want him to see my car. So I turned around facing out and parked down the street. I walked closer to make sure it was his car, and it was. He had parked in the back next to her car in the parking lot behind the apartment building. I walked back to my car and left then."

"So when did he come home?" asked Ralph growing ever more concerned now. The audacity of this guy cheating on his little girl really disturbed him. He emptied his cup then got up and fixed another cup of coffee for himself, the same way as the two previous cups.

"He came home about seven in the morning," said Judy.

"So, he spent the night with her," Ralph was angry and getting more angry by the moment.

"I was already up, drinking coffee," Judy said in a low voice. She was getting tired. She was emotionally drained at that point from just talking about it.

"What did he say," asked Ralph, "was the reason he was gone all night?"

"He said he worked all night, that he ran into a problem that he couldn't get resolved. He said that it took him hours, but that he finally figured it out, fixed it, and then could come home."

"What happen then?" asked Ralph in his attorney voice.

"He said he was tired and was going to bed." Judy repeated sounding upset and on her last straw.

"So he lied, and you caught him in a lie. And he is cheating on you. Well, that's grounds for a divorce." Ralph exercising his lawyer skills pressed on.

"Yes, he lied to me, and he is cheating on me." Judy said in a sad voice. She was sad and angry that her dad forced the truth out of her.

"Did you get pictures of him walking her to her car; better yet, did you get a picture of his car parked next to her car at her place."

"Well, no I did not have my camera with me," said Judy thinking who thinks of that when you are emotionally upset.

"We need proof," insisted Ralph.

"Can't I just divorce him?" Judy asked not really wanting any more drama in her life.

"I think he should be caught in the act," said Ralph. The whiskey in his coffee was having its effects, and it was taking its toll. Ralph was becoming belligerent and revengeful.

"Why?" asked Judy.

"Judy, you must be mad," Ralph said.

"Yes, I am mad — and sad." Judy said in tears, "I wish none of this was happening."

"So where is he now?" demanded Ralph in a sharp tone practically cutting her off. He was mad and wanted to get the bastard.

"He says he is stuck at work with all the snow and that he can't leave because of the roads. He can't leave, and no one can get there to relieve him. So whoever is there needs to stay. They have enough food and everything there, so he would be all right. He said that he has to stay at work until the roads get cleared enough for the relief electrician to drive to work and for Alan to be able to drive home."

"So do you think he is really at work?" asked Ralph.

"No, I do not. I think he is at her place. I think he got there right before the snow started and is still there." Judy said sounding upset.

"So, stuck at work and probably for three days, is what he told you?" her father asked.

"Yes, that is what he said," Judy said, but she did not believe her husband. She just knew the guys at Alan's workplace were trying to cover for him. She was being made a fool of, and she didn't like it, and she knew her dad really didn't like it. Alan will soon find out that she was not the quiet shy docile little girl he thought he married. But for a moment Judy did feel a slight pang of guilt. She had after-all trapped Alan into marriage by faking a pregnancy. But she was willing to put that aside for now, since she discovered he was no better than she was, and that he lied too.

Chapter Seventeen

It was Monday the first day of February, and according to the *Belleville News Democrat* and television news, the snowfall had nearly ended. So far levels were reaching a total of twenty-four inches in some areas. Snowplows were scheduled to work all of Monday and Tuesday into the night so people could hopefully get out and go to work by Wednesday morning.

Alan was getting antsy and was ready to head home. He enjoyed spending the three days with Dawn. It was very relaxing at first, having all the sex they wanted, drinking a gallon of Rosé and watching cable movies on HBO. Dawn was glad that she had gone to the grocery store right before the big snow and had enough groceries to cook meals for Alan and herself.

In a way they were both sorry to see the snow begin to melt and their three days together end. But both felt you can only lay around for so long and it was time to get back in their normal routines. Dawn knew she would miss him, but she also knew that she would rejoice once again for being thrown back into her single lifestyle routines. She missed Nancy. And as if right on cue, as Nancy was thinking about her too, the phone rang. It was Nancy calling to check on her again.

"Hey, how are you guys doing?" asked Nancy sounding cheerful as she always did when she heard the sound of Dawn's voice. She was eager to talk. She needed to take a break from Gerry, so she called Dawn from her bedroom on her Princess phone while he was watching some sports show on the television in the living room.

"So are you guys having a good time together these snow bound days?" asked Nancy with a smile in her voice that Dawn easily picked up and felt a slight pang in her stomach. She didn't want Nancy to be happy for her regarding Alan; she wanted Nancy to be jealous and to be able to hear it in her voice. But Nancy was happy that Dawn had Alan and that she had Gerry.

"Yes, three days and a gallon ofRosé," giggled Dawn, "it has been very nice." She wanted to exaggerate just a bit.

"Gerry is busy next Friday evening helping his brother move to his new apartment if the roads are cleared enough. And if they are do you want to meet me at Panorama? That band we like so much is back in town and playing there Friday evening," Nancy said.

"Sounds great," Dawn answered eagerly, "I'll plan on it." She knew Nancy could hear the smile in her voice. She wondered if she had a crush on Nancy because Nancy paid extra attention to her, or did Nancy paid extra attention to her because she was easily available. She wasn't sure.

Dawn had a problem with accepting affection and love from anybody; for some reason, it just did not register with her. She always thought lesser of herself. She saw herself as loving but not as being loved. She guessed it was because her mother was cold and her father was present but indifferent, cruel and emotionally distant. No kisses, no hugs while growing up. Dawn thought that you just have to come to terms with your life circumstances on your own; that is, after you figured out the reason you were like you were in the first place. In the meantime, Dawn vowed to just be her own best friend. She was doing fine. Alan was her lover and Nancy added the welcome spark of joy, so she looked forward to whenever they got together.

"Alan is working Friday evening, so that will be great," added Dawn. "I'm sure he will stop into Panorama after he gets off of work." Dawn was happy their plans were set. She had missed one on one time with Nancy. She liked double dating with Nancy and Gerry but enjoyed their special one on one times when just the two of them did things together.

Chapter Eighteen

It was Monday and the snow was still deep in many places so Greg and Wanda decided not to venture out in it. They were sitting around watching television and talking. Wanda wondered how Alan and Dawn were fairing staying at Dawn's apartment for three days. Greg wasn't sure if he should ever tell Wanda that he saw Alan with another woman at the home show several weeks earlier. Greg had to admit that he was no angel either so why bring it up; but still it was hard to keep such an intriguing secret.

Greg was bored with the movie he and Wanda were watching and as he sat there pretending to be watching it, his mind began to wander. He thought about the day a week or so back when he saw Alan's car parked at Tim and Joe's. It was after he had seen Alan at the home show with another woman. Greg was curious. So when he drove past Tim and Joe's and saw Alan's car parked there. he couldn't resist and stopped in for a beer and to visit with Alan.

"Hey, how's it going?" asked Alan sitting at the bar near the door. Greg heard Alan's voice coming from the bar even before his eyes could adjust to the dim light of the smoky bar.

"What's up?" asked Greg. He was glad to see Alan sitting there alone and with a full glass of beer which meant he wasn't about to leave. Greg was hoping that they would not be interrupted by anyone because he wanted to talk to Alan alone. Alan motioned for him to sit down and Greg sat on the stool next to him.

"I just got off work," responded Alan then carefully lifted the very full glass of beer to his lips to take a sip.

"You worked the day shift today too then," commented Greg. Greg worked at Granite City Steel as a welder inspector. He liked the job; it was easy enough and the pay was good.

"Yep they called me in. They were shorthanded on the day shift today. Tomorrow I'll work evenings again," answered Alan.

"Yeah, I know I have been working shift work too," said Greg.

There was a slight lull in the conversation as Greg drank his beer, and Alan finished the one he had and ordered another one. Greg could not get seeing Alan at the home show off his mind. He wondered how he could bring it up, but Alan gave him an opening.

"So what else have you been up to?" asked Alan.

"Well, I am trying to help my mom remodel her kitchen. You know trying to get some ideas for her. She doesn't know what she wants. I tried to get her to go to the home show with me, but I ended up going by myself," responded Greg

"Did you see anything interesting there?" asked Alan then taking a sip of the full glass of beer the bartender just sat in front of him.

Greg almost burst out laughing while taking a sip of his beer. He practically choked on it and thought, like hello I saw you there with another woman, that should have been interesting enough in itself. But Greg controlled his desire to laugh even though it was becoming difficult not to, since the beer was beginning to have its effects going straight to his head. He wanted so much to say — "Yeah, I saw you with your wife and that seemed pretty interesting to me." It took all his will power to restrain himself.

"Why you looking at me like that?" asked Alan looking Greg up and down.

"What do you mean, Alan?" asked Greg.

"You look like the cat that caught the mouse or something, however the saying goes," egged on Alan.

"Well, I did see some interesting kitchen designs, even have a contractor coming over to speak with me and my mom about some plans."

"What else?" asked Alan, and then laughed suspecting what Greg was about to say.

"What's so funny?" Greg said beginning to laugh himself.

"You saw me there, didn't you?" Alan said feeling his beer and wanting to brag a bit about having two women in his life. He loved the suspense and excitement it conjured up in his soul.

"Maybe, I thought I saw someone who looked like you," Greg just had to play him. "Who were you with?"

"I was with Judy," Alan said sheepishly

"And Judy is…" Greg egged on, feeling very curious.

"My wife," finally admitted Alan sounding as natural as could be but looking a little sheepish having been caught in the act. He realized that he did care what his friends thought about him, but he doubted he would ever change his ways.

"Oh, I see," Greg teased., "I didn't know you were married."

"Well, I am," admitted Alan as he lifted his glass to take another sip.

"Does Dawn know?" asked Greg looking Alan straight in the eyes.

"What?" laughed Alan in a devilish laugh. "You don't tell your girlfriend that you have a wife. Come on, I know you know that, Greg." Alan wanted to have something on Greg too in order to keep his own secret safe.

"Yeah, you're right," smiled Greg and motioned to the bartender to bring them each another beer.

"Am I right?" asked Alan feeling rather proud, and without guilt regarding the matter.

"Yeah, you're right. So what were you guys looking for at the home show?" asked Greg, and they both burst into laughter at Greg's attempt to change the subject.'"

"Oh, Judy wants to redo the kitchen and the bathroom, so we were getting ideas. Her ideas will cost a bundle, but her dad has tons of money. He bought the house for us. Of course, he pretty much picked it out too; and its right up the street from where he lives, of course. He likes to keep a close watch on, Judy, his precious daughter."

"So aren't you a little nervous," asked Greg, "I mean about dating Dawn. What if the old man catches you?"

"Ralph Burns," chuckled Alan feeling the beer go to his head, "he's an old man; he's no threat."

"Ralph Burns, the lawyer, who used to be the big shot prosecuting attorney of St. Clair County, that Ralph Burns. Man you got some nerve," smirked Greg.

"Ah, he's just an old guy," Alan laughed; he wasn't afraid of an old guy like Ralph. Alan liked to tempt fake. Fact was, he wanted out of the marriage, but didn't really want to give up the super nice house, expensive vacations, her money, their fancy lifestyle, or Judy's trophy winning good looks. Judy and Alan both drove Mercedes that her dad bought for each of them. Of course, Alan liked the Mercedes but did not want to drive it to work, so he bought the secondhand Volkswagen to drive back and forth to work. He felt the Mercedes was a bit too obnoxious and perhaps there was a slight pang of guilt of driving an expensive car your father-in-law paid for as you cheated on his daughter. After all Alan wasn't totally without a conscious.

"You might want to be careful," warned Greg. He was beginning to get a little concerned about cavalier and overconfident Alan.

"Oh come on, you worry too much," suggested Alan as he watched the worrisome expression shade Greg's normally smiling face.

"Just warning you," smiled Greg in friendly fashion

but was dead serious. In his mind Alan was indeed playing with fire.

"Let's have another beer. Hey, this conversation is just between you and me, right?" Alan asked and wanted to be sure his secret was safe.

"Oh, for sure," agreed Greg "I am not saying a word to anyone, certainly not to Wanda. She couldn't keep a secret if her life depended on it. Which reminds me I guess I better leave soon and make this my last beer. We are going over to her folks for dinner this evening. Wanda wants to get married."

"Well, there you go," Alan smiled.

"I'm not sure if I really want to settle down just yet and have a kid like she wants. The whole idea frightens the hell out of me."

"Tell me about it," added Alan sharing Greg's concerns.

"Next time—gotta go," Greg said after he emptied his glass then got up from the bar stool and patted Alan on the shoulder as he turned toward the door.

"Yeah I have to leave too,' said Alan checking the time on his watch.

"Going to Panorama after work on Friday like usual." Greg paused to ask Alan before he headed to the door.

"Yep, I'll be there," waved Alan, "see you then." Alan emptied his glass then and got up to leave too. He knew Judy was waiting for him and probably had dinner ready. Dawn was on the back of his mind then, but he'd see her at Panorama Friday evening. He loved his life and the two women in it. But even with two women in it, he felt that something was missing. He told himself that he couldn't have it all so be happy with what you have.

Chapter Nineteen

Alan drove straight home. He enjoyed pulling in the driveway of their big fancy house.

"There you are," greeted Judy as Alan came through the kitchen door.

"Hey Babe," Alan smiled and kissed her cheek.

"I have dinner in the oven. Are you hungry?" she said as she greeted him with a kiss trying to put aside her anger and jealousy and play along with his cheating scheme. She smelled beer, but that was normal. Alan always stopped on his way home for a couple of beers — to unwind he always said, so she stopped asking.

Judy's emotions were torn when she saw him. She was always glad to see him in spite of his philandering ways. He was smiling, he was happy, and he was handsome. She had to admit to herself that they were the reasons why she fell for him in the first place. But down deep she had a nagging angry feeling she tried very hard to suppress. She wanted to trap him and catch him in the act to prove to him that she was no fool. She had her pride. She knew what he was up to. She followed him once and she planned on following him again. She had her camera all ready. She could be just as sneaky as he. She played it up. She would be extra nice to him to keep him off guard. He had no idea she suspected he was messing around on her.

"This is delicious," Alan said sitting at the table eating pot roast, mashed potatoes and gravy with mixed vegetables.

"Thank you, my dear," Judy smiled taking a sip of her wine.

They sat talking casually about this and that, her work managing three beauty salons and his work as an electrician at Monsanto. Alan commented how nice it was for Ralph to come by and check on things while they were at work.

"Yes, Dad has to micro-manage everything," Judy pointed out.

"Your dad's a character all right," laughed Alan. "I know he is very precise and particular. I know I certainly had to pass the test when you and I were dating."

"Oh yeah, that's Dad," Judy agreed, "always looking out for his little girl." The best was yet to come she thought, just wait till I get some pictures. She felt a smirk forming on her lips. Two can play this game she thought. I will not be a push-over. After all I tricked him into marriage didn't I, and that part of it worked didn't it, she got him. She vowed this affair would be his last affair.

Although, when she saw that girl the night Alan walked her to her car, Judy had to admit that there was something about her and thought that she was sexy and cute. Judy tried to ignore that fact and out of jealously she told herself that she had it all over that girl, whoever she was. Of course, Judy was just telling herself all that to make herself feel better. But if Judy was honest with herself, she had to admit that her husband's girlfriend was very cute and sexy, and found that she felt a stirring just thinking about her.

After dinner, although Alan felt rather tired, he lured Judy into the bedroom. They had sex and she fell asleep in his arms. He laid awake for a few minutes thinking that he almost called Judy Dawn at one point. He'd have to be more careful.

He didn't know why he cheated, it was in his blood he figured. His stepdad had cheated on his mother all the years that they were married. Finally his stepmother had had enough and took his hunting rifle and shot him in the chest when he came home late one night. She told the police she thought he was an intruder, but the investigators weren't buying it. She was terminally ill with cancer at the time so she figured she had nothing to lose. She just had enough of his cheating ways. She died before her trial date was set. At the time, Alan was already a young man and out of the house living on his own. He lost both of his parents within a few months. He laid in bed wide awake in the dark listening to Judy breathe deeply next to him, in his arms. He did love her. She was beautiful.

Chapter Twenty

It was a Friday evening just a few weeks before the big snowstorm was to hit the area. It had been a long workweek, and Dawn looked forward to Friday evening when the group would gather at Panorama. It was just a given that if you were out and about, no matter what event you attended you ended up at Panorama.

"Having the usual, a glass ofRosé?" asked the barmaid.

"Yes, I believe I will," Dawn said as she looked around the crowded bar and dance floor for Nancy. She stood at their usual place at the bar. They had always positioned themselves at the end of the bar on the way to the restrooms. It was convenient for them because of the crowded place and sooner or later everyone went to the restroom, so they got a chance to check out everyone in the place, and strike up a conversation if they thought fit.

As she took a sip from the glass of wine the barmaid sat before her, she spotted Nancy dancing with Dennis, and she knew it was his favorite song he liked to dance to. It made Dawn smile to see her friends having fun. She loved her friends and the way they referred to themselves as "the group." The group is going on a hayride, or the group is going to Jeff's party.

There were at least thirty friends who hung out together and they were all single. There is safety in numbers thought Dawn and loved her single life but knew that most in the group dated and planned on marriage someday, but not her. Single was safe she thought. Her parents never got along, she grew up listening to daily arguments at every meal, no hugs, no kisses, just hateful fights. So that was what Dawn thought marriage was all about, and she had seen enough fighting growing up and did not want to live through any more of it or be under some man's thumb. Marriage seemed foreign to her and very unlikely. Besides she dated men but had crushes on women, so just how mixed up and messed up was that?

"What about your friend," asked the barmaid when she came around again, "do you think she wants another scotch and water?"

"I would say yes," offered Dawn. She watched as the attractive barmaid went about her business to fix the drink. As she watched the barmaid, Dawn felt an ache in her heart knowing she would never have that; that which she wanted so badly. It was like window shopping at an expensive store with no money, so never getting to buy anything because it was so far out of reach. She loved the sweet soft kindness of feminine women. She was distracted then as Nancy returned to the bar stool next to her.

"Oh, she brought me another drink," Nancy

remarked slightly out of breath from dancing the swing with Dennis.

"Yes, she did," Dawn said.

"Did you get it for me?" she asked Dawn. She had been dancing with "fancy moves" Dennis, to "Towering Inferno" by the BeeGees and she was hot, perspiring and thirsty.

"Yes, I did," Dawn smiled again.

"Oh, great she brought me a glass of water too," and held the cold glass to her forehead before taking a big drink. The icy cold felt as good against her skin as it did going down her thirsty throat.

"Thanks, he's such a good dancer, I'm so thirsty," Nancy said still out of breath as she lifted her glass to take another sip. "I could barely keep up with him; but it was fun."

"You two were great. You followed his lead very easily and looked like you were having fun out there dancing the Shag." Dawn took in the beauty and charm of her friend as the wine took its effect on her empty stomach. Dawn hadn't eaten too much lately; she had been dieting, so she could get in her skinny jeans. Someone had told her eating a half of grapefruit before every meal would curb her appetite and melt the fat away. She was sick of grapefruit, she would have to try something else next time or just give in and buy a bigger size.

"I need to dance, this wine is hitting me already," laughed Dawn. Dennis heard her say that as he reached between them to pay the barmaid for his beer.

"Come on then," he laughed, "it's your turn." He set his beer down on the bar and took Dawn's hand. He gave her a look that asked if she was okay with that. Dawn nodded as she got up from the stool to follow him to the dance floor. She loved dancing the Swing to "Brown Eyed Girl" by Van Morrison. They had a great time dancing. Dennis was busy the rest of the evening with everyone wanting to dance with him.

"Hey, you going to Jeff's house party next weekend," asked Nancy when they had a chance to talk.

"It's Friday isn't it?" Dawn asked. "Yes, Gerry is doing something with his brother beforehand, so do you want to ride with me if Alan is working?"

"Sure, that would be great," Dawn felt her heart swell. She would look forward to Friday. She was happy.

Greg and Wanda came in then, they had been to a movie.

"What movie did you see?" asked Nancy.

"ET," believe it or not," smiled Greg, "A little too sweet for me, I prefer movies like 'Alien' with Sigourney Weaver, but Wanda liked 'ET.'"

Before they knew it half the group was there, talking, laughing and dancing. About eleven-thirty Alan came through the door, spotted them and made his way through the crowd.

"Alan's here," announced Nancy to Dawn, feeling no pain and leaning on Gerry.

Alan worked his way up to the bar. It always made Dawn's heart feel good when he came in the door and headed directly for her without stopping to talk to anyone. It's the little things Dawn thought. She knew they would have a couple more drinks and when the place closed, they would head back to her place and have sex and he would stay the night and leave early in the morning like he always did. But before he left they would make their plans for Saturday evening, when he would return. Of course, he would stop along the way at the bars. It was their routine and it suited Dawn just fine.

Chapter Twenty-one

It was one-thirty and closing time, Dawn and Alan both were feeling no pain as they all began leisurely departing their favorite Friday night meeting place. Everyone was heading home or down the street to an all-night diner for breakfast ,but Dawn and Alan were heading to her place.

"I'll follow you," Alan said as he walked her to her car. He had parked next to her. Neither of them saw the woman sitting in the dark colored car several parking spots away. Judy was seeing red, she was so angry sitting there in her car watching Alan with his girlfriend. She was determined to catch him in the act. She had her camera in hand ready to take pictures.

Judy made sure the flash was off, so they wouldn't see it, as she snapped a picture of Alan giving Dawn a quick kiss as he opened her driver side door for her. Judy hoped there was enough light so the pictures would turn out okay when she got them developed.

As Dawn, followed closely by Alan, pulled out of the parking lot, Judy kept an eye on the direction they were headed. Traffic was light this time of night, and they were easy to follow. Judy just had to make sure she stayed far enough behind as to not arouse suspicion. Dawn's apartment was only about three miles from Panorama, so they pulled up at her place after only a few minutes.

When Dawn and Alan pulled around to the back of her apartment building to park their cars, Judy sat and waited for them to walk around the building to the front door. Judy parked down the street and had her lights and engine off. She could easily make them out as Dawn unlocked the door. Alan was all over her almost undressing her as she tried to turn the key to unlock the door. Judy watching from a safe distance, zoomed in with her camera lens. She hoped the light at the apartment front door was bright enough to get her picture. The door closed and no living room lights came on, so Judy assumed Dawn and Alan probably headed straight to the bedroom. She wanted to get a closer look.

Judy got out of her car and crept quietly up the street. She crossed the ditch onto the front lawn of Dawn's end apartment then quietly walked around the building to the back. She listened at the bedroom patio door, but she did not hear anything. She only saw their two cars parked in the rear lot parked close to Dawn's bedroom patio door. The back patio light was turned off and Judy was glad of that, otherwise she was afraid they would see her walking around.

Suddenly Judy's temper, much to her surprise, got the best of her when she saw the handle to the patio door, and she yanked on it to open it. Inside Dawn laid awake and listened to Alan snore. Alan had fallen asleep and was snoring lightly and did not hear the commotion at the patio door but Dawn did.

Dawn had sat up quickly frightened out of her wits. She thought she saw a strange figure at her bedroom patio door looked like they were trying to get in. She froze with fright. She couldn't move for a second. Only when she saw the figure slip away out of sight could she regain her nerve to move. Dawn wondered if someone had the wrong apartment. There were six apartments in each building and six buildings. She thought of waking Alan, but he was sound asleep and besides the dark figure wandering outside the patio was gone.

Dawn eventually fell asleep and forgot about the incident so by morning she didn't mention anything to Alan about seeing someone yank on her patio door handle. Later on when Alan had gone and she thought of it again, she had to laugh out loud thinking the woman was probably out drinking like she had been and came home confused and went to the wrong apartment.

Dawn really didn't know her neighbors that well, it seemed there were always tenants moving in and out. As she rode with Nancy to Waterloo on Saturday she thought of it again and told Nancy.

"Sounds like something I would do," laughed Nancy as she drove the winding highway south out of Belleville towards Waterloo. It was a pretty day and they were enjoying the drive. Nancy's aunt had a nice lunch prepared for them and they had a great visit.

Dawn learned how to play Euchre, a fun and fast-moving card came. Dawn had to remember, right and left, bar, jacks were higher than aces and could trump aces. They played several hands then Dawn really caught on and even won the last two.

Nancy and Dawn enjoyed their afternoon together and with Nancy's aunt and uncle. They talked about how much fun Nancy's aunt and uncle were on the way back to Belleville. And of course, they talked about their guys too. Dawn could tell that Nancy wanted to talk about Gerry, and she had something on her mind regarding Gerry's wishes.

"Gerry wants to spend more time with me." Nancy shared her concern. "He thinks we should live together." Dawn's heart sank but she tried to sound cheerful.

"Well, that certainly sounds like fun," mused Dawn but she was actually more than a little disappointed. Dawn worried and wondered if Nancy would still be able to meet her on Friday evenings, and if they would still be able to spend Saturday afternoons together.

For some reason the song "Another One Bites the Dust," by Queen, popped into her head and she couldn't get it out of her mind. It was a song she usually thought of when any of their friends ended up getting married. Dawn, a true, bachelorette was always sad to see one of her friends leave the world of freedom that she herself so enjoyed.

Being free meant making your own decisions, and Dawn loved that. Like death, Dawn always hated to see them go and leap into the dark abyss of potential marital pitfalls. She wanted everyone to enjoy being single like she did. Dawn enjoyed her carefree life going to bars and house parties, she didn't want her life of fun to end. She liked making her own decisions, doing what she pleased, and hanging out with the group. Dawn noticed when friends got married, it was like they dropped off the face of the earth never to be seen again. But it was typical, she was the odd one. She would just enjoy the group for as long as there was a group.

"It's his idea," Nancy said happily, "his apartment lease is due up soon and he wants to move in with me."

"Well, they say, two can live as cheaply as one," Dawn was actually surprised to hear her voice sound that cheerful, it certainly did not match the dull ache in her heart.

"Well, I don't know about that," responded Nancy, "Gerry has no sense for managing money."

"Well, I'm happy for you just the same." Dawn congratulated her. Dawn had always figured that one day Nancy and Gerry would move in together. Dawn too was afraid that her one on one time with Nancy, like this, would come to an end. But Dawn had to face it, most people were not like her and most people wanted to get married and settle down with a lifelong partner. Dawn was glad that Alan thought more like her. He always agreed with Dawn and told her numerous times that he loved her but did not want to be married, and she was fine with that

Chapter Twenty-two

The next Friday evening Alan met Dawn at Panorama as usual, and when the bar closed, he followed Dawn to her place. The next morning Alan left Dawn's apartment and drove home. He tiptoed inside the house. He quietly slipped into bed and curled up next to his wife just as it was getting daylight. He was happy Judy was a very sound sleeper, and that he could sneak into the house without waking her up. He could hear her breathing deeply next to him.

He looked at her for a long moment in the dim morning light and realized that he did love her. He loved Dawn too. And he thought that if there were more hours in a day, he could love a third woman. He loved the secrecy and sneaking around which made him feel alive and much younger than his thirty-nine years.

Alan had to figure out how he was going to sneak out of the house to go to Jeff's party with Dawn that night. Jeff's parties were very popular and lots of people always showed up. He wanted to go. He planned to have his buddy at work page him after dinner, then he would tell Judy that he had to go to work. He was excited. A plan was in place for his great escape into the night for a fun evening.

Chapter Twenty-three

It was Saturday, a week before the unexpected big snow blizzard was about to pounce on the St. Louis and Belleville area and blanket it in twenty-four inches of snow bringing the area to a halt.
The night of Jeff's party had finally arrived. There was a certain electrical energy charge in the air, as if change was about to come and everyone's routines would be interrupted.

Everyone was ready to party. It promised to be a big affair. There were cars parked around the corner and up and down the street in front of Jeff's house. Alan said he had to work for a while, and Gerry was busy doing something with his brother so they both told the girls they would meet them at the party. Dawn rode to the party with Nancy, and the guys would join them there later.

"Great party, Jeff," Dawn smiled as she and Nancy finally made their way through the crowd of cheerful talkative people who kept stopping them to chat. They had spotted Jeff and caught up with him in the crowded living room where a bar was set up.

"I love throwing parties, and I'm glad you could

make it. Isn't this great!" Jeff said, he was happy to see them there.

"This is great, Jeff," Nancy said looking around at the crowd of people there then added, "you throw the best parties."

There were lots of people meandering all over the house and out back on the patio. There were people everywhere. Dawn saw many familiar faces as well as not so familiar ones. She was excited, loved to party and see old friends, and meet new ones.

The evening was filled with laugher and great conversation. Later into the evening, Dawn spotted Alan through the crowd and saw that he had stopped to talk with Jeff. Alan and Dawn smiled at each other from across the room as they each were caught up in conversations but knew they would share what they learned later on the ride to Dawn's place. Dawn spoke with Greg and Wanda for a bit, lingered near Nancy and Gerry. Dawn just naturally gravitated toward Nancy and Nancy toward Dawn. They always did, no matter where they were, they ended up hanging out together. Many friends were there, including Rosie and Barry, who Dawn had not seen for a long time since they had moved out into the county. She was eager to talk with them.

"Oh, we just had to come to town, we couldn't miss Jeff's party," Rosie bubbled so happy to see everyone. Barry and Rosie had moved onto a farm near Okawaville, Illinois, about an hour's drive from Belleville. They showed pictures and talked about getting everyone out their way soon for a party.

Dennis was on a date with Deb from Collinsville whom he had dated several times before. Deb had invited her two friends Sherry and Joann, and they were having fun meeting everyone. They all three lived in Collinsville and shared their stories of the community wanting to preserve the historical huge Brooks Ketchup bottle water tower.

It stood tall and high up in the sky along route 159 on the right side of the road as you come into Collinsville. It had been a standard landmark in Collinsville since 1949. There was talk of tearing it down after a drunk ran into one of the steel support legs and did lots of damage. The company wanted to tear it down but since it was such a landmark, like the huge Standard Oil sign near Forest Park on Highway 40 and Clayton Road in St. Louis. They decided to take up a collection to restore and renovate it, and the project was very successful.

The people of Collinsville had taken up collections and signed petitions to preserve the Brooks Ketchup tower. As the ladies told the story, they all laughed about a tow truck driver who could not locate the accident when the guy ran into it. They determined that the tow truck driver must have been new to the area because everybody knows where the giant Brooks Ketchup bottle is in Collinsville, and if you don't know exactly where it is located that you just have to look up from almost any direction and you'll see it.

"The Brooks ketchup bottle is so huge how could he not see it?" Deb asked laughingly."

"Well, it makes for a good story," Joann responded.

Dawn and Nancy had met Deb, Joann and Sherry at previous events, and they became good friends. Sometimes just the ladies hung out to celebrate birthdays or enjoy weekends stays at the Holiday Inn at the Lake of the Ozark's. They gathered at one point that evening and re-hashed their drunken, joyous trip to the Ozark's they took together.

They laughed when they reminisced about Deb getting so drunk and the others thinking she had wandered off in the night in the woods. They couldn't find her and they were worried Deb was so drunk, as they were, that she may have fallen over the balcony railing of their room and tumbled down the steep wooded hillside. They talked over what they should do to find her, and they worried till they heard a low voice say, "I'm over here on the couch, you knuckleheads." They laughed all over again at the joyous moment when they found Deb laying on the couch. She had merely laid down to take a nap, and they in their wine induced imaginations thought that they had lost her forever.

"You ladies are crazy," laughed Dennis as went to get refills on his and Deb's drinks. Dawn wasn't feeling any pain as she laughed and chatted with Nancy, Deb, Sherry, and Joann. Then Dawn spotted Alan across the room and she tried to make eye contact again as she did earlier when he was talking to Jeff; but this time he was busy talking to a woman Dawn didn't know.

The woman was strikingly beautiful with red hair and eyes that Dawn imagined were clear blue as she could see from across the room. It looked like Alan knew her very well. If Dawn didn't know any better, she would have thought that they were arguing. Dawn saw Alan laugh then and guessed maybe the pretty woman was mad at her man and telling Alan all about it.

"Who is that woman Alan is talking to?" asked Nancy when she saw Dawn watching him.

"I don't know," said Dawn, "but she sure is pretty, isn't she? There was just something about her that struck Dawn and made her heart beat fast.

"Yeah, I guess," Nancy smirked in a way Dawn had never seen her do before—almost as if Nancy was jealous at the way Dawn was looking at the woman.

"Aren't you a little worried about Alan talking to her?" asked Nancy looking at Dawn rather strangely.

"No, actually I'm not worried about him talking to her," replied Dawn, "I must say that I am surprised that I'm not worried. Personally, I think I would like to know her myself."

"I'm jealous," smiled Nancy "I thought I was your one true love."

"Oh!" Dawn replied a little surprised at Nancy's playfulness, "There's room for two isn't there?"

"Why whatever do you mean," Nancy decided to play along. But only for a moment as Gerry returned just then with another drink for her. Dawn always thought that Gerry seemed jealous when Dawn was around Nancy, and she felt she was never left alone with Dawn for very long. It was as if Gerry sensed Dawn's feeling for Nancy even though Nancy may have never had a clue about how Dawn felt.

The night was getting more exciting as everyone drank more and dance music played. At one point Dawn went to use the bathroom, and the door wasn't locked so she entered. She was shocked at the sight before her. There was Greg laying on his back on the floor and a woman slightly familiar to Dawn only because she had seen Greg talking to her several minutes earlier. Were they having sex? As Greg laid on his back the woman straddled him. Much to Dawn's shock the woman was screwing a half passed out Greg who had a big smile on his face.

"Holy crap," was all that Dawn could muster to say as she quickly backed out of the bathroom and quietly closed the door. They didn't see or hear her, and Dawn was glad. Dawn stepped back into the hall and went to another bathroom which was vacant, much to her relief. As she opened the door to leave the bathroom Nancy was heading in and ran into her.

"There you are," said Nancy her face right in Dawn's. Before Dawn knew what was happening Nancy was kissing her — on the lips.

"There's that kiss I knew you wanted," teased Nancy, "don't tell Gerry." Nancy smiled and Dawn was floored with delightful surprise.

"Nice kiss," Dawn finally admitted after she caught her breath. "Of course I won't tell Gerry," a flustered Dawn agreed as her heart beat at a rapid pace in her chest.

"How about you and I on the side," inquired Nancy as she watched the look on Dawn's face transform from one of shock, to the look of fright, to finally settling on a sweet smile that almost made Nancy laugh.

"Actually, I would like that," Dawn replied whirling with pleasure.

"Sorry, can't, Gerry would kill me," Nancy said with a smile.

"Damn, you tease. I'm sorry to hear that," responded Dawn. She was serious and knew that Nancy was not. She was just playing her to see what Dawn would do. Nancy enjoyed the kiss though and told Dawn as much. But Gerry was soon to move in with Nancy and he wasn't messing around on her and she didn't want to mess around on him. Dawn was disappointed.

"Well, as long as we remain friends," Dawn said as Nancy kissed her on the cheek which made Dawn's heart feel all warm all over again.

"I need a drink and a Tareyton 100," said Nancy with a smile and a wink.

"I'm right behind you," laughed Dawn, as she followed Nancy to the bar.

Dawn and Nancy headed for the bar Jeff had set up near the kitchen area where a friendly bartender happily served them. They got their drinks and decided to meander through the crowd and step out on the patio to have a smoke.

Walking toward the patio with Nancy, Dawn saw that Alan and Gerry were headed their way. Dawn spotted them before Nancy did, and thought well I can't have her to myself for a single moment, but at least I got a kiss. Gerry came up with a smile and put his arm around Nancy. Dawn smiled at Alan as he came up behind her then kissed her on the cheek.

"Wonder what is wrong with Wanda?" reported Gerry as he stood next to Nancy, Dawn and Alan.

"Why do you ask?" asked Nancy

"I was just out front and saw Wanda kicking in Greg's car door, and then I saw Greg running after her. They argued a bit and then Greg opened the passenger side door and pushed her in the car, and they left in a hurry."

"Well, isn't that something," was all that Dawn could say trying to sound surprised. She decided not to tell anyone what she saw going on with Greg and the woman in the bathroom. She was more interested in knowing who the pretty redhead was that Alan was talking to earlier, so she asked him.

"Who was that pretty lady you were talking to?" asked Dawn without commenting further on what Gerry said about Greg and Wanda.

"Oh, her," answered Alan looking just a bit uncomfortable. "She is a friend of mine's girlfriend. Well, ex-girlfriend I guess you could say. They were arguing. She was pissed at him." Alan was lying sure as hell; she was no friend's girlfriend. Alan only said that because he knew Dawn probably saw him arguing with the woman.

But what really happened, much to Alan's shock and surprise, was Judy had decided to follow Alan to see if indeed he was going to work that evening. Alan had no idea and was totally surprised when he saw her come into Jeff's party. He was only too glad that he was standing next to Jeff, and not Dawn, when Judy walked up to him.

"Well, where did she go," asked Dawn "did she leave?"

"Yeah," said Alan looking around a bit, as if looking for her. "I think she must have gone."

The party went on for another hour or two until the last of partying people either decided to stay the night or leave and go to breakfast at an all-night diner. Alan and Dawn decided to just go home to Dawn's, as Gerry and Nancy said they were just going to go home too and not out to breakfast.

Alan and Dawn chatted on the way to her place about who was at the party and who they got to talk to and what was going on with them. It was a great party and they guessed there had to be at least eighty or ninety people there. They both agreed Jeff's parties were always fun. They both were a little lightheaded when they got to Dawn's apartment, but made love and fell fast asleep.

Chapter Twenty-four

The morning after Judy had followed Alan to Jeff's party, Ralph made his daily visit to Judy's house. Judy told him all about what she did, how she followed Alan to the party. She told her dad, how Alan had the audacity to go to Dawn's afterward and not come home.

Of course he told Judy at Jeff's that he had received a page from work. He told Judy that he had to go to work to fill in for the midnight shift guy who called and wasn't going to make it in. When Judy walked out of the party, she did not leave but sat and waited in her car. From a safe distance down the street, she kept Alan's car in her sights. She watched and when she saw Alan and his girlfriend leave the party and get into his car, she followed them. Judy wanted to know for sure that Alan lied to her earlier, and just as she suspected he was not intending to go to work like he had told her. Her dad was appalled when he heard Judy's tearful story.

"I'm going to kill him," Ralph said angrily as he poured himself a cup of coffee. With his back to Judy, hiding his flash, he quickly poured Irish whiskey into the strong black coffee. He quickly slipped the flask back into his jacket then turned to sit opposite Judy at the kitchen table. As soon as the coffee cooled a bit, Ralph drank down the much-needed strong concoction which was more like three-quarters whiskey topped off with a one-quarter cup of coffee. He was becoming more bold, and was getting to the point where he no longer cared if Judy could smell the whiskey on his breath. Of course, Ralph did not think that he had a drinking problem and an anger problem that was over taking him and destroying his good judgement.

"No, Dad," cried Judy as he sat down across from her, "please no violence, he is not worth going to jail over." Judy knew her dad had a temper and was suddenly sorry that she even mentioned Alan's lying tactics to him.

"The nerve," smirked Ralph, "the bastard, lying and cheating on my little girl."

"Dad, I knew I shouldn't have told you," admitted Judy.

"Where is the bum now?" asked Ralph.

"Her place I assume," said Judy. She was tired of arguing.

"And the girl was at the party too?"

"Yes," answered Judy, "she was there."

"Well why didn't you go after the girl?" insisted Ralph.

"I will go after her in time," said Judy, "I didn't want to make a huge scene and spoil the party for everyone."

"You should have pulled her hair out," smirked Ralph "want me to take care of her too, along with Alan?"

"Dad!" Judy was beginning to become concerned. It seemed that since her mom died her dad just didn't seem right anymore. He was overprotective, and belligerent ever since her death.

Judy was seventeen when her mother died after losing her battle with cancer. Her dad sued the hospital, the doctors, and the drug companies for malpractice. He thought that they miscalculated her treatment dosages, they were too strong, and therefore lethal and therefore hastened her demise. She was throwing up body tissue and right away Ralph knew the dosages were all wrong and too strong for her. He had not been the same since her tragic death.

"I have a gun," smirked Ralph pouring himself a half a cup of Irish whiskey and topping it off with coffee. He was feeling pretty intoxicated, and thought he better ease up a bit on the booze.

"Dad," Judy knew her dad liked to exaggerate and carry on, and didn't mean things he said in the fit of anger. She hoped he was all talk and no action this time too as far as Alan was concerned.

Judy was heartbroken and felt lost. It was time for her to get her life back together. These early morning coffees sitting with her dad and complaining about Alan had to end. She needed to pull herself together and get her life straightened out. She was grateful that she had her work to keep her busy.

She owned and managed three hair salons, and styled hair part time at one of them. It was time to get back into action and participate more in her life and not just sit and worry about what Alan was up to. But Alan worked on her nerves and made her mad.

The audacity of him being mad when she followed him and approached him at the party. The nerve of him! He is cheating on her and then gets mad because she confronts him about it. How rude! It was why she turned around and left the party. She just figured she'll catch him in the act and confront him again. She was becoming even more angry. Judy wondered if she should have complained to her dad about Alan after she saw how it upset him and that he was drinking more. Judy was concerned for her dad but she had no idea just how crazy her dad would become with anger at the fact that Alan was cheating on his baby girl.

Chapter Twenty-five

Alan and Dawn made love. Sex was always good after a party when both Alan and Dawn were light-headed with good conversation, laugher, fun and alcohol. Alan fell asleep afterwards, but Dawn laid awake listening to his light snoring as she thought of Nancy's kiss and how sweet it was and how it stirred her.

She had had Nancy on her mind when she made love with Alan. She wondered how it would be if it were Nancy in her arms instead of Alan. Her imagination saw a flicker of red then as she wondered how the pretty red head would be like to kiss. There was no denying it. Dawn may have dated men, had sex with men, but in her heart, she wanted a woman. Oh, she loved Alan, and sex was satisfying enough but somehow there was a void. Something was missing. Dawn knew what it was—it was the soft, gentle touch of a woman. She knew it and she felt it in her heart and soul.

Lying there thinking she suddenly became very sad because she knew Nancy would never be in her life like that, not that way. The hour was late, and Dawn still felt the effects of all the drinks she had had at the party. Slowly she drifted off to sleep and she dreamed about the red headed beauty see saw at the party. In her dreams she made love to her and it was wonderful.

Chapter Twenty-six

Alan and Dawn woke up early the morning after the party still feeling a little hung over. Dawn wanted him to stay in bed with her but Alan was getting dressed and preparing to leave to go home. As Dawn kissed him good-bye, she again wondered why he never asked her to come over to his place. It bugged her, and so she brought it up again as he was leaving.

"I could come over to your place sometime, you know," suggested Dawn matter of factly. She meant it was only fair that she drive his way once in a while.

"My place is such a mess," Alan had to think fast, "you don't want to see my place, Dawn." Dawn looked at him rather strangely he thought and so he had to come up with something for her that at least sounded like an invite.

"Let me at least clean up the place first, okay," he added and tried to sound embarrassed by admitting he was sloppy.

Ah, that worked he thought thinking that the excuse he gave about being messing at least gave him some stalling time. But he knew sooner or later Dawn would expect to see where he lived. As it were, he always tried to avoid the issue. He never mentioned his place and vaguely indicated that he lived in an apartment in Villa Hills. It was the only thing he could think of fast and remembered there were apartments just down the street from his and Judy's house.

Actually, it was just Judy's house, it never really felt like his house. Her dad bought it for them, but mainly for Judy. Alan felt like a guest most of the time. Her dad was always there getting in their business. Her dad lived down the street and walked over most days. Alan just figured he would be there most days, if not in the morning, usually for dinner. The house was big enough he could have just moved in with them. But Ralph Burns being the prominent attorney that he was had to show that he was very successful and had lots of money. So he lived in the biggest house in the subdivision, a proud symbol of his success.

Chapter Twenty-seven

It was a typical Friday evening and Nancy was eager to meet up with Dawn at their usual Friday night meeting place.

"Hey girl, you going to Panorama tonight?" she asked Dawn. It was a busy week and finally it was Friday and time to swing.

"Hi, Nancy," Dawn was always delighted to hear Nancy's cheerful voice. "You bet, count me in."

"Great I'll see you there then," Nancy was happy to be going out that evening with her friend.

"What are you wearing this evening?" Dawn asked Nancy. Nancy was always buying something new to wear every week.

"Remember, I bought that cute little top to wear," Nancy loved shopping every payday at the new K-Mart store near her apartment off of 74th Street. She liked to take Dawn with her when she went shopping.

"I remember, it looked really good on you."

"Oh, you just say that, cause you like kissing me when we're both drunk," laughed Nancy.

"Yes, I do like kissing you when we are both drunk," Dawn had to laugh in return. She wondered if Nancy really knew how much she did like it. Did Nancy feel the same way?

"Okay, gotta go, my boss is wanting me in his office," whispered Nancy, "I'll see you tonight."

Dawn was all excited. She was happy that she was going to get to see Nancy at Panorama. One of her favorite bands was scheduled to play music so she would have to wear her best dancing shoes. She could count on the group showing up and Dennis and several of the other guys loved to swing dance as much as she did. Alan would be getting off work at eleven and he said he would see her there as usual.

Chapter Twenty-eight

"Is Alan at work?" Judy's dad asked when he called from his office.

"Yes, he should be, I guess, I have been too busy to call there and check today," responded Judy.

"What have you been doing?" he asked and actually sounded interested in hearing how her day was going.

"I just got home from working at the salon, and checking on my other two salons," she answered happily feeling proud of her successes.

"You're doing good," said Ralph sounding like a loving father, "I'm proud of you."

"I must admit, I am doing pretty good," Judy boasted adding, "all three of my salons are proving to be very profitable."

"So what are you up to this evening?" her dad asked.

"Well, I'm going back to the salon later this afternoon. I will do a client's hair and makeup before her big award presentation this evening at Fischer's Restaurant."

"Well, that sounds great," said Ralph with a smile in his voice.

"Yes, she is potential walking advertisement for me. So, if I do a great job she should bring in more customers," Judy smiled thinking about her client and the hair style she was planning for her. Judy had been feeling much better lately since her businesses were striving.

"So, Dad what are you up to this evening?" asked Judy hoping her dad would get out and have some fun.

"Well, some friends are going out to dinner, and I decided to join them. I'm sure we'll sit around afterward, have a few drinks and chat. So, I am looking forward to it."

"That's great, Dad," Judy said, "have a fun time."

"I plan on it," promised Ralph. Ralph planned on having a great time all right, he planned on getting drunk. The cases he had been working were coming to a close and with the trial outcome he had hoped for, so he was ready to celebrate. He planned on getting plastered.

Chapter Twenty-nine

"Hey Ralph, we have the table in the corner," his law partner Jim Hopkins told him when he greeted him at the door. They were at Fischer's Restaurant on West Main. It was a very popular place for attorneys and businessmen. The evening was going well as Ralph's law partner and his wife brought along Alice, a newly divorcee and she and Ralph hit it off the moment they were introduced. There were four couples and if one person wasn't ordering drinks, another one was.

There was a wedding reception in one of the reception halls. They could hear the music from inside the restaurant area. Ralph and Alice found that they couldn't resist and decided to crash the reception and danced a few dances. They had fun dancing the polka and trying their best to dance the Lindy Hop. Ralph was just drunk enough where he was limber and loose but not too drunk to not remember his groovy moves as he led Alice all around the dance floor. Alice was a good partner and could easily follow his lead. They had fun dancing to Bobby Darin's "Mack the Knife, and then Glenn Miller's "In the Mood." They laughed as they glided all over the dance floor.

Everyone was having a good time, and no one wanted the evening to end so as they were leaving Fischer's everyone said they were going to stop by Tim and Joe's and have a nightcap, so Ralph and Alice joined them.

They have great conversation along with a few drinks. Ralph and Alice planned to see each other again and made plans for the following weekend. As Alice and Ralph's law partner and friends were leaving Tim and Joe's, Ralph saw his old law school buddy, Mike, come in the door, and so he stayed and had a drink with him. As they chatted, Ralph soon realized that Mike was drowning his sorrow with alcohol. He told Ralph the story of how his ex-son-in law ruined his sweet little daughter's life.

"That jackass did nothing but cheat on my little girl," complained Mike getting quite upset.

"So, what happened?" asked Ralph growing more interested since his own little girl also had a cheating husband.

"Well, she got sick and nearly died," said Mike in a low sorrowful tone. "I don't know if that jackass poisoned her or if just his mean-spirited shenanigans broke her heart and worried her so that they made her ill. Maybe it was both."

"So she finally divorced him?" asked Ralph.

"Oh, she divorced him all right," said Mike with a bitter tone to his voice. "Oh yeah, he signed those divorce papers all right, after I beat the living hell out of him."

"You beat him up?" asked Ralph with the sound of delightful intrigue in his voice. He was getting so drunk he was beginning to slur his words.

"Sure did," Mike said with an evil grin.

"Really, Mike," Ralph repeated again. He found his friend's gAlant gesture to protect his daughter very admirable. That's what a good father does Ralph told himself. He protects his daughter.

"Oh yeah, a father has to protect his little girl," insisted Mike, "I beat him within an inch of his life. Yeah, I caught him in the act with another woman. I really wanted to kill him, but I didn't."

"So did the law come after you?" asked Ralph.

"Oh, hell no, besides like you, I am in good standing with the judges. You and I we are in court every day and we know the judges. We know how they can be too, don't we?" and Mike laughed a grand gesture of a laugh like it was their little secret alone about how the judicial system really worked. You scratch my back, and I'll scratch yours was a common practice, and everyone in the courts system knew that.

"Yep, you know you got something there," agreed Ralph and he got to thinking about his own little girl and that miserable husband, Alan, that she had. Alan was never home; he was never there for her. She made her own living, she had him, her father, so she didn't need him.

"Well, I better get going home, the wife is waiting," said Mike as he looked at his watch then began to get up from the table.

"Heading home then?" Ralph asked not really ready to leave just yet himself.

"Yeah, I'll see you around. Come in more often. I'm here all the time," said Mike before he headed out of the door.

Ralph had just ordered another drink when his friend Mike got up to leave, so sat there thinking to himself while he drank it. The more Ralph drank the more intoxicated he became, and the more angry he became as he pondered his little girl's situation with her cheating husband. The fact that Ralph had no one to go home to, like Mike did, bothered him too. He was feeling sorry for himself and angry at life for having no one. Oh, he had a date the next weekend with Alice and he was looking forward to it. They would double-date with his law partner Jim Hopkins and his wife. Jim and Ralph had their own story, but he didn't want to think about that now.

He missed his dear wife Susan. She understood him. Why did his wife have to get cancer and die and leave him, Ralph wondered? He was too drunk and too angry for his own good, but he did not realize it. The more he drank, the more he felt like picking a fight with someone. It was getting late and Tim and Joe's was near closing, but he wasn't ready to go home to an empty house just yet. A thought popped in his mind. Maybe he would head over to Panorama Lounge isn't that where Judy said she sat in the car on a Friday evening and watched Alan leave Panorama with that woman. Brilliant idea! He quickly downed his drink and headed out the door to his car.

Feeling no pain and staggering just a bit, he left Tim and Joe's got in his car and very carefully drove to Panorama. He parked just as some folks were leaving Panorama and walking to their cars. He sat quietly in his car in the dark and waited and watched the door. He had no idea Judy was parked several rows over in the back of the parking lot doing the same thing. She did not see nor recognize his car, nor he hers. Neither was expecting the other to be there.

Ralph watched the door closely to see who was leaving as many couples were heading out to their cars. Finally, Ralph saw Alan walk out the door with a woman. He watched as he walked her to her car. Then Alan quickly walked to his car got in and followed her out of the parking lot.

"Oh no," Judy said out loud to herself when she saw her dad's car several rows over. She quickly pulled her car in front of his and blocked him. She jumped out and went to his driver side window.

"Just what do you think you are doing?" she demanded when he rolled down his window.

"Keeping an eye on him," slurred a drunken Ralph seeming surprised to see Judy there.

"You are drunk, Dad," yelled Judy, "get out of the car and get into my mine now."

She had never spoken so harshly to her dad before and the sound of her own angry voice scared her. Who was she becoming, she wondered. She was already mad at Alan for being with that woman and now she was even more mad at her father for being there and for being drunk. She got him in her car after persuading him to leave his car there and that they would come back and get it in the morning.

"Let's follow them," suggested Ralph slowly and clumsily getting into Judy's car.

"Look I know where she lives and I know what he is up to, so I do not have to follow them. We are going home."

"Well this isn't over yet," yelled an irate and drunken Ralph.

"Come on dad, we can always follow them home another time," encouraged Judy. She wanted to get her dad home.

Chapter Thirty

Unbeknownst to anyone that it was coming, the record-breaking blizzard was just a few days away. It was to be the blizzard that no one knew was coming and it would come with a vengeance.

Ralph nursed another hangover, he had lots of them lately. Judy ate chocolates when she wasn't busy managing her three beauty salons. She scarfed them down and left candy wrappers all over the house.

Chapter Thirty-one

Then came the weekend of the big snowstorm that buried the city and surrounding areas. After two days of being cooped up in the house. Ralph was getting antsy.

Ralph could not take it anymore. He knew Alan was cheating as he was snowed in at his girlfriend's place and not at work. This was the third night Alan was over at his girlfriend's place. He knew his baby daughter had to be in real emotional pain. Being at home alone while her cheating husband lied to her about being at work, and being at his girlfriend's instead.

Finally, Ralph decided that he had had enough and drove his big truck over to Judy's. It was late evening and dark out except for the illumination from the snow lighting up the night.

"Come on, we've going for a ride." He could see Judy had been crying and he found empty chocolate candy wrappers laying all over the house.

"Where to?" asked Judy looking through swollen eyes from crying all weekend. She was sad about her marriage and sad about being stuck inside going stir crazy in a snowstorm all alone by herself in that big house.

"You are going to lead me to that woman's place, where your cheating husband is staying," he demanded.

"I don't know if that is such a good idea," Judy worriedly responded.

"Oh yes, it is," insisted Ralph, "come on get your boots and coat on. We are going. You sat around here long enough crying your eyes out."

Judy was reluctant but then went along with his idea. She sat in the passenger seat of the huge four-wheel drive pick-up truck and nervously watched the all-encompassing white scene that surrounded them and covered everything as they cautiously drove on the slippery roads. She was nervous and constantly reminded her dad to drive slowly as she gave him directions to Dawn's place.

The snow was so deep, they could not make out where the side of the road ended and the curb and ditch began. There was no one on the roads but them and it felt erie to them. In the distance they could see the lights of an adventurous snowplow driver and it looked like he had his hands full attempting to maneuver in the very deep snow.

The roads were packed deep with snow but Ralph's big high-profile four-wheel drive pickup went through the snow and deep drifts with little difficulty. It took them awhile because the streets were not cleared very well if at all. It looked like one clearing pass was attempted and the snowplow came up. They drove along in silence mostly, concentrating on trying to see where the road was. The big truck slipped several times but they managed to stay on the road. They were the only ones on the road so they ran the four-way stop at Freeburg Avenue, where they slipped a bit but the four-wheel drive gripped and the truck plugged along. Ralph carefully and cautiously made the slight turn left onto George Street and about halfway up the hill, Ralph backed the truck around so it was headed west out on the dead end street for a quick getaway. He parked the truck and turned the engine off. Ralph reached under the front seat of his truck and felt around until he found his revolver.

"Hey, what the hell is that?" demanded Judy. It was the first time nervous and upset Judy had said anything other than giving him driving directions.

"I just want to scare him, okay?" Ralph was angry and a little surprised at the sound of his own voice.

"Oh Dad," but she jumped out of the truck after him and nearly fell to her knees in the deep snow. But she managed to keep her balance and hurried to follow him as he took big steps. The night was deathly quiet, more snow had fallen, and the very deep snow cover acted as quiet insulation. Without speaking, they quietly trudged along as best they could. The night was cold, dark and silent. The only sound was their breathing and the sound of their boots crunching into the deep snow.

Ralph carried the gun in his right hand. Knowing her dad had a gun made her very uncomfortable, but like the obedient daughter that she was, she followed right behind him. They cut across the apartment complex yard to the back parking lot at the end of the long one story building. Judy followed Ralph as he trekked around the snow-covered cars parked in the back lot until he came upon the familiar car which was Alan's. His car was parked near the patio door of Dawn's apartment.

Suddenly, feeling lightheaded and breathing heavily from trekking in the snow Ralph, hesitated at the patio door. As if making a sudden impulsive move, Ralph yanked on the patio door handle with his left hand still holding the gun in his right. Judy stood in disbelief and shock. She couldn't believe he actually yanked on the patio door handle. She thought they were just there to look around.

They both were stunned, when much to Ralph's surprise the patio door jerked open under his forceful pull. Ralph figured the patio door would be locked and his intent was to scare the hell out of the two lovers inside. But, much to his shock when he jerked the patio door handle, the patio door flew open making a huge racket and letting a burst of cold air into the bedroom. In the darkened room, two very startled people suddenly raised up to a sitting position at the loud sound on the slamming open patio door.

"Holy shit," a surprised Ralph yipped as he suddenly was shoved forward. Judy suddenly lost her balance and fell into the back of Ralph pushing him forward. Ralph then tripped on the bottom metal ridge of the patio door frame and the gun he carried fired into the darkened bedroom.

Dawn screamed and Alan yelled as they both felt sudden sharp pains in their bodies. Dawn screamed at the intruders who were stumbling around trying to get up off the floor.

"What the hell," yelled Dawn! The room was dark but the streetlight at the back corner of the parking lot lit the background enough for the two intruders to be seen. Ralph had yelled and Judy had screamed when the gun went off twice in rapid fire as her dad tripped over the patio door sill. At first Judy thought her dad shot himself and fell but soon realized that he had tripped, fell down, but was not shot. Judy was filled with sudden dread and for a moment didn't know if she should run, cry or scream.

"Oh no," said a frantic Judy when she heard the woman in bed scream and begin to cry. She heard nothing from Alan. She wondered what condition her cheating husband and his girlfriend were in as she suddenly felt a sense of panic.

"Damn," mumbled Judy almost tripping over her dad scrambling around on the floor in the dark looking for his gun.

Dawn was crying and had the sheet pulled up around her. She felt a sticky wetness and instinctively knew it was Alan's blood on the sheets next to her where Alan lay in quiet stillness.

"Oh my god," Judy heard a frantic little girl voice say. Judy scrambled pass her dad near the foot of the bed, as he was trying to get up from the floor. In the dim light, Judy could see that Alan looked to be shot dead.

To her shock and surprise, she felt nothing. In a frantic state Judy went toward the whimpering sound she heard. She felt a sense of dread as she realized the life and death situation she and her dad had created. This was no television show or love crazed movie, this was real life gone horribly wrong. Her dad had just shot two people, the gun, fear, pain and the blood were real.

"Oh my god what just happened," asked Dawn, "who are you?"

"I'm Alan's wife, Judy."

"Wife? Oh my god, what?" A wide-eyed shocked Dawn stared in the dim light of the room, "I didn't know."

In an instant Judy realized that the woman was innocent and did not know that Alan was married. And in a heartfelt moment Judy put her arms around Dawn. For some reason Judy felt the need to comfort this poor unsuspecting woman.

"Alan's wife?" Dawn asked in a voice that sounded sad and full of disbelief. I had no idea. My god, Alan!"

"The gun just went off," managed a frightened old man on his hands and knees trying to get up from the floor. "I didn't mean to shoot them."

"Oh, this is not good," Judy was a bundle of mixed emotions. She was frightened, in a panic. Her crazy dad had just shot her cheating husband and his girlfriend. Judy didn't feel sadness or sorrow seeing Alan lay there on the bed covered in blood. She was fixated sitting on the edge of the bed holding a shaken young woman who apparently did not know that Alan was married.

"I had no idea he was married," cried Dawn over and over again, "he said he was divorced. I'm so sorry." She cried as Judy held her close. There was something about this young woman that touched Judy's heart and she wasn't sure why, but she did not want to let her go. Maybe because this young woman, like her, was sharing some of the same pain that Judy had been feeling all along.

While holding Dawn, Judy felt the wall in the dark and reached up until she found the light switch and switched on the light. In the light Dawn had to turn away from Alan's blood-soaked body and as she looked up she saw the red hair and blue eyes of that pretty girl that Alan had talked to at Jeff's party.

"You're her," whispered Dawn through tears, "You're the girl I saw speaking to Alan at Jeff's party — you're his wife?" Dawn had to know.

"Yes, widow now apparently," Judy said in a flat tone as she wrapped her arms tighter around Dawn's small body. Judy was not surprised that she did not feel much of anything looking at Alan's bloody body. Maybe she was in shock she thought.

"I'm getting sick," said Dawn, "my stomach."

"Let me help you," whispered Judy and she gently lifted up Dawn, sheet and all and helped her through the bedroom doorway right around the corner to the bathroom only a few steps away. Dawn leaned against the sink as Judy grabbed a small cup and poured some water for her to sip. As Judy held on to Dawn in the bathroom, she could hear a commotion in the bedroom, as police and a neighbor who called them, came through the bedroom patio door into the bedroom.

Suddenly there were lights and cops and people everywhere in the parking lot. The police had their guns drawn and told Ralph to drop the weapon or we'll shoot. Ralph dropped the gun and put his hands up high into the air.

Dawn felt raw with emotions, naked and bare, with only a sheet wrapped around her as police looked around the apartment. Judy sensed her discomfort and quickly went and gathered Dawn's clothes that laid on the bedroom floor and took them to the bathroom and helped Dawn put them on and that was when they realized that Dawn had been shot too. They could hear the police lead Ralph out of the bedroom to a police cruiser as the two ambulance attendants carted Alan to the ambulance. Judy heard a police officer tell the neighbor that the victims involved were lucky that the fire department had a four-wheel drive ambulance.

"This must be awful for you," a frightened Dawn said to Judy, "I'm so sorry,"

"Trust me, you weren't the first," Judy sounded sad as well as angry, "actually I feel numb where he is concerned."

"I feel horrible," cried Dawn in Judy's arms. Somehow they found comfort in each other. Suddenly Judy pulled away a bit, and took Dawn's face into her hands, looked deep into her eyes, then kissed her full on the lips. Dawn kissed her back. Dawn had never felt anything like what she was feeling just then ever before. She had been mesmerized by this woman's beauty when she saw her from across the room at Jeff's party that night speaking with Alan. They looked more like they were arguing, no wonder. She was right, they were arguing and Judy had something to be quite disturbed about. In that moment, Dawn felt she never wanted to leave Judy's arms. She felt at peace.

"I'm feeling weak," Dawn heard herself say, "and I'm bleeding all over."

"Oh my gosh," said Judy, "that's not only Alan's blood on the sheet that was yours too. You've been shot."

Dawn almost passed out and began sliding out from Judy's arms toward the floor. Dawn was bleeding from her side.

"This woman has been shot and she needs an ambulance," Judy yelled to the police. They had just put Alan in the ambulance and heard Judy scream so were racing back inside the apartment to get Dawn.

Dawn laid on the floor as the ambulance attendants brought a gurney to the back-patio door of the apartment.

"This one is still alive too," said the attendant to the driver, "let's get them to St. Elizabeth's hospital, it's the closest."

Chapter Thirty-two

With Dawn and Alan both unconscious in the back, the ambulance driver drove to the hospital. Judy watched it drive away as she sat in her dad's truck for a moment in silence in order to grasp what had just happened. What just happened she thought. My dad just shot two people. My husband is a cheating jerk who could be dying. And there is something about his girlfriend that moved my soul to such an extent that I kissed her. Perhaps it's the fact that we were both cheated on. Maybe it was the pain and the hurt I saw in her eyes. Judy didn't know what to think, her heart was racing. Alan had no family to notify; well not that Judy knew of. He was such a secretive kind of guy Judy wasn't sure anymore. Someone should be notified that Dawn was shot and in the hospital.

The only thing Judy knew to do was to drive to the house where she had followed Alan to the party weeks earlier. So she drove to Jeff's house and parked the truck on the street, walked up the sidewalk to the front steps and knocked on the door. It was early morning and getting daylight. She figured she would probably be waking him up. Jeff was famous for having parties nearly every weekend and the house and yard had the shambled appearance that a weekend long party was still in the process. Soon someone came to the door and opened it. It was a man, fairly short, with a thick black mustache. His hair was messed up as if he had just gotten up or never went to bed. His jeans and a white long sleeve shirt were wrinkled. He held a cup of coffee in hand as he opened the door with a curious expression lighting up his smiling eyes. A look that said the party was still going on, so come on in, you don't have to bother to knock.

"Hi," greeted Jeff as he opened the door.

"Are you Jeff?" asked Judy.

"Yes," Jeff responded with a friendly smile. He thought she looked slightly familiar. Oh yes, the woman Alan argued with a few weeks back, who could forget this gorgeous red head.

"I stopped by your party not long ago, one night to speak--well, rather argue, with my husband, Alan," explained Judy in a nervous sounding voice. Jeff quickly picked up on her nervousness and figured something was wrong.

"Sure, I remember seeing you," smiled Jeff, "but only for a few minutes. Of course, I remember you—your red hair." Jeff remembered thinking she was strikingly lovely. He had looked for her later on but couldn't find her. He had asked Alan where the beauty went and realized now that Alan lied by saying she was a friend of a friend or something to that affect. Jeff remembered Alan being rather vague about it. Well, I guess if you plan on cheating on your wife, you don't want unsuspecting possible future mistresses to find out. So this woman is Alan's wife, and Dawn is his girlfriend. Jeff wasn't really surprised, this kind of thing was fairly common with his friends.

"How can I help you?" asked Jeff sounding concerned.

"Well, something awful has happened," Judy said with tears in her eyes.

"Oh, my what," exclaimed Jeff, "a car accident?"

"I wish," said Judy and Jeff looked at her strangely, "well, a minor accident then." Judy didn't know what she was saying; but there was no time to take it back and she thought, the heck with it and went for the real reason of her visit.

"My dad and I went to Alan's girlfriend Dawn's place last night to spy on them. My dad had a gun with him and well; she hesitated, not wanting to admit it, he shot them both," said Judy. Saying it out loud suddenly made the truth hit home, and the horror of it all hit her like a ton of bricks, and she let out a sob.

"Oh my god," remarked Jeff in disbelief.

"They were both hurt pretty bad; Alan the worst maybe so it appears. He was unconscious." She was rambling and she knew it.

"Take your time," urge on Jeff, "tell me more."

"Alan was shot and unconscious. Dawn was shot and conscious at first then she passed out. She may have internal injuries, both were taken to St. Elizabeth's Hospital."

"Oh my gosh," repeated Jeff as his tired eyes suddenly woke up and grew large with the startling news.

"Yeah, it's awful," cried Judy

"How can I help?" asked Jeff.

"I don't know Alan and Dawn's friends," Judy said wiping tears, "so I came by here in hopes you could tell them what happened."

"Well, I certainly can," said Jeff, "my gosh how awful. I'm so sorry. Is there anything I can do for you? Can I get you some coffee?"

"No thanks, I'm fine, I'm just letting the truth sink in, I'll be okay." Judy thanked him again then turned to leave.

She was in a daze. She knew her dad would be all right, and she knew he knew that too. He had enough friends in law enforcement and the county court system to get him off. Judy didn't know where to go next. Her father was with the police and Judy knew that he knew the police chief and the judges and with his attorney status he would be home soon. She wasn't worried about him, only unset and mad that he did such a thing.

She was mad and upset with herself too for not stopping him and taking the gun away as soon as she saw that he had one. But like the obedient child she was, she followed his lead; his lead that led to two people getting shot, and for this she was very sorry. Judy drove to St. Elizabeth's Hospital. She felt numb as she asked registration and admissions about Alan and Dawn's condition and if she could see them.

Chapter Thirty-three

The nurse at registration told her that Alan, her husband, was down the hall in operating room three and had been in surgery since he arrived. She didn't know his immediate condition. Judy lied in order to get the information about Dawn.

"And miss, your 'sister' is still in surgery also," said the nurse with a twinkle in her eye knowing only family members were allowed and that it was common for people who came there to see patients to be relatives, even if they were not.

"She is in the next operating room, number four. I haven't heard any updates on either one of them yet."

Judy had time to ponder her thoughts and her feelings as she sat in the waiting room. She loved Alan, she guessed, but more as an angry friend now, certainly not a wife. She was numb, sad rather than mad. When it came down to life and death, she couldn't be angry with him for cheating, after all she had her faults too. She cared about him. In her heart she knew he would be okay.

Judy was worried about her dad but knew he would come out all right in the end. Somehow they would figure out how you can accidentally shoot two people. Something else bothered Judy. She wondered about her intense feelings for Dawn. When she followed Alan and Dawn to Jeff's party that night, she really had no idea who Dawn was, because Dawn wasn't standing with Alan at the time she approached him; he was talking with two guys. She wondered how it would had been if Dawn would have been standing right there with him that night. She would never know.

Judy only realized her heart ached now for Dawn. There was just something about her; something about her sad eyes and her innocence. Judy had believed Dawn when Dawn said that she didn't know Alan was married. And Judy knew Alan all too well to know that he loved to sneak around. Alan should had known that Judy's dad wasn't going to put up with Alan's philandering ways. In a way she felt part of the blame for Dawn and Alan getting hurt. She never should have complained about Alan to her dad. He was drinking more lately, and she knew it. She should have known that sooner or later he would go off half-cocked and do something crazy.

Chapter Thirty-four

"Excuse me," called out the nurse from her desk behind the window to Judy sitting alone in the waiting room.

"Yes," Judy turned and looked; she was anxiously awaiting an update on the two patients.

"Dawn is in the recovery room, if you would like to see her," reported the nurse, just as the doctor came into the waiting room to give Judy an update.

"We got the bullet out of her okay. We had a little trouble stopping the bleeding, but we got it stopped. Luckily the bullet missed all major organs. She should be awake soon," reported the doctor, then continued, "and she will be hurting a bit so we'll give her some pain meds. Will you be the one taking care of her?"

"Yes," Judy heard herself saying. Her heart jumped at the possibility of taking care of Dawn.

"That's great," said the young doctor, "if she has you to change her bandage then she can go home tomorrow. She'll need at least three days of bed rest before she tries to get up and be active. Walking around the house several times a day for short periods of time will be fine. And she probably won't need the pain pills by tomorrow, but we'll send them along anyway."

The doctor had no progress or prognosis report to tell her anything about Alan's condition. He said another surgeon would be coming out to update her on him.

So Judy just figured she would have both of them at her house. She wanted Dawn there but Alan she did not. She could easily be at home to help Dawn recover because she did not have to leave her home in order to check on the salons she managed, they pretty much managed themselves. She called Alan's work and let them know what had happened. Alan's co-worker expressed his concern and said he would inform the boss and that the boss would be calling her for an update.

Judy was eager to go into the recovery room to see how Dawn was doing. She looked forward to taking her home with her to care for her.

Chapter Thirty-five

When the police realized it was Ralph Burns, the former St Clair County prosecuting attorney, who did the shooting, they pretty much figured he would get off without any charges. So they went easy on him from the beginning. Judy realized her father had a lot of pull in the community and had favors owed him, so she wasn't worried about her dad being prosecuted and sent to prison. She knew the mayor and most of the judges were good friends with her dad.

The local paper wrote an article stating it was an accidental shooting. The story in the paper sounded confusing to Judy, that somehow Alan, Judy and her father were visiting Dawn. Ralph had heard someone at the back-patio door and thought it was an intruder. He just happened to have his gun with him. He stepped outside and looked around. He heard someone running away the report stated. He found no one, turned to come back through the patio doors and tripped over the patio door bottom metal strip as he was coming back in. The gun went off and shot Alan and Dawn who were standing close to each other. It was declared an accident. Case closed.

Chapter Thirty-six

"Hi," was all that Dawn could manage through her pain and her heart jumping in her chest when she saw the blue eyed, red haired beauty step into the recovery room where she lay recovery from surgery.

Dawn's heart melted at the concerned look in Judy's eyes. She wanted Judy close to her. Dawn could not forget how it felt when Judy held her in her arms at her apartment after she was shot. Somehow she felt a connection, a bond had formed between them. Dawn knew that Judy felt it too. They had a cheating man in common, that was true, but there was something more Dawn could sense it and knew that Judy could too.

Judy stepped closer to the bed and said nothing only leaned over and kissed Dawn's forehead and Dawn's heart melted. If only this woman knew how she touches my heart Dawn thought. Dawn was at a lost for words when Judy took her hand.

"I am taking you to my place and taking care of you," Judy said as she kissed Dawn. When Dawn was about to say something, Judy added, "And I won't take no for an answer." Dawn could only smile. She was about to say something more when the surgeon for Alan came into the room.

"Your husband will be fine and make a full recovery," smiled the doctor as he spoke to Judy.

"That is good to know," replied Judy. She did not want Alan to die, she only looked forward to the day she would be divorced from him.

"He just needs a few days of rest and probably light work duty for a while when he goes back to work. No heavy lifting until his wound heals. I told him that. You can go in and see him now. He's in the next recovery room."

"Thank you, doctor," smiled Judy, "I'll go in and see him then."

"Only stay a minute," ordered the doctor, "he is still coming out of anesthesia and he'll be sleepy anyway. I'll check on him later and he can probably go home tomorrow morning."

Dawn's doctor came back in then to check on her and to him she appeared to be doing fine.

"Since you have someone to care for you," said the doctor, "I think you can go home in a few hours." Judy nodded standing next to Dawn's bed and holding her hand.

"I'll check on Alan and be back in a minute," Judy smiled at Dawn after the doctor left the room. Dawn felt Judy's tenderness and it made her want to cry.

As soon as Judy walked out of the room, Nancy came through the doorway.

Chapter Thirty-seven

"My god, what happened," Nancy asked with a worried tone to her voice, "are you okay? Jeff told me what happened. Deep snow or not I took Gerry's Jeep and managed to get here to see how you were doing. How are you doing?" She asked sounding very concerned.

"I think I'm fine," Dawn said. "Yes, I think that I am going to be fine," Dawn smiled feeling dazed from the shock of being shot, the dozy effect of pain pills and the sudden emotional twist in her relationships. She was happy to see Nancy.

She was surprised by her feelings though. Nancy was her good friend whom she had had a crush on—until Judy came along and threw her off balance by her kisses. In one tragic event her romantic life took an unexpected twist. Dawn's head was spinning, somehow now her crush on non-participating Nancy was moved to the back of her heart's love chamber, and Judy's affections were moved up to the front.

"Who was that woman leaving your room?" asked Nancy sounding rather annoyed already knowing the answer.

"Judy, Alan's soon to be ex-wife," replied Dawn her heart beating faster just by saying her name out loud.

"Oh, the red head," smiled Nancy, "I just saw her leave your room. I remember seeing her at Jeff's party now. That's Alan's wife?"

"Yes, I had no idea he was married," Dawn said, and she didn't. She believed him when he never took her to his house because he said it was such a mess that he was embarrassed to have her there. Most men are messy she thought, but thinking back about that, she thought that most men do not care if you see their messing places. So she should have doubted him, but she guessed it was easier not to, and besides, she reflected back to the old adage that love is blind.

"Is she pissed," asked Nancy sensing possible gossipy drama to take back to the group, "with you for dating Alan?"

"No, I didn't get that at all," Dawn smiled thinking of Judy's sweet kisses.

"Why, what," wondered Nancy, "why are you smiling?"

"'Let's just say I like Alan's taste in women," Dawn said quietly not wanting to give it totally away. But a part of her wanted to let Nancy know what Nancy had missed out on and could have had with Dawn.

"I see," replied Nancy with a doubtful tone to her voice.

"She knows, and more importantly believed me, when I told her that I didn't know Alan was married."

"Where does Alan stand with you?" asked Nancy

moving closer to the bed to hear Dawn better and to get a better look at her for herself to see how she was doing.

"Well, I should have known he was married," whispered Dawn. "In all the months we dated, he never once took me to his place. That should have been a real clue to me. I mean I love the guy—but it will be different now—more like a distant friend. I just can't be mad. I know I should. The idiot almost got me killed."

Chapter Thirty-eight

Judy walked the short distance down the hospital hallway to the recovery room where Alan was. She thought that she would see a drugged up sleepy guy in pain.

"How are you doing, Alan?" asked Judy. It took all the emotional energy she could muster to be halfway civil to her cheating husband. Just like Alan to be sitting up in bed, all smiles as if he never did anything wrong.

"Can you ever forgive me?" asked Alan, more sorry he got caught than about hurting her or Dawn. Down deep he was sorry his father-in-law was mad and figured he would never see any of his father-in-law's money in the future. Alan was sorry about that because he enjoyed the fancy lifestyle Ralph had provided for him. Well, he guessed he blew that, but he just couldn't help falling for and dating other women.

"No actually this time I do not believe I can forgive you," Judy said speaking softly, even though she was angry as hell and wanted to yell at him.

Alan thought, fine, Dawn will have me. I won't be alone. Dawn will have me. He felt he needed to go into Dawn's hospital room and see how she was doing. To make sure she was all right. It never occurred to Alan that cheating on his wife had put Dawn's life in danger and she may had been killed. Alan being rather full of himself and egotistical never thought that Dawn may be angry enough to never see him again.

"You look like you are doing fine," observed Judy. She thought that she would have rather seen him suffering a bit more than he appeared to be. She thought that some serious pain and suffering for a while, at least, would do him good. He deserved to hurt after the pain he put her through by cheating on her.

"Well, yes I am doing pretty good," said Alan, "the doctor was just here and said that just a few days of rest and I'll be able to go back to work." Alan just assumed that Judy would want to take care of him. He was that self-confident and sure of himself. Judy would describe him as egotistical and narcissistic, but even if she told him what she thought about him he wouldn't hear it anyway, he was so full of himself.

"Well, maybe your friends or one of your co-workers will let you stay with them until you are up and able to go back to work and find yourself a place to live."

"You're kicking me out?" Alan was shocked at the thought. Immediately he thought of a back-up plan, that he could stay, rather move in, with Dawn. Dawn would take care of him he was sure of it.

"Of course, you have to move out," said Judy rather sarcastically, "that is unless you want my father to finish you off, and shoot you dead next time."

"What?" proclaimed Alan and his eyes grew larger than normal. It never occurred to Alan that Judy's father may still have it in for him and finish what he set out to do. Alan had it in his head that the shooting was an accident, just like the newspaper article stated that he read in the morning's paper.

"Yeah, I don't think it would be safe for you to come back to the house," Judy wouldn't say the word home. There was no home there for him. And besides Judy was going to put the moves on Dawn, so Alan couldn't have her either, and that made Judy smile. Judy knew that Dawn fell for her by the way she kissed her that night and that convinced her. What better way to get back at her cheating husband then to steal his girlfriend. Two can play at this game, she thought.

Without another word Judy turned and walked out of Alan's hospital room leaving him open mouthed and staring in disbelief. He thought for sure if he got caught cheating that Judy would forgive him, but no such luck. Judy up and walked out on him. Alan suddenly felt all alone; that is, until he looked up and saw Greg standing in the doorway.

"Hi Greg," said Alan, "good to see you."

"Hey good buddy," greeted Greg, "how are you doing?"

"Oh, physically I'm fine, I guess," Alan said with a sad tone but was very glad to see Greg's warm friendly face.

"Kind of got yourself in a mess, hey?" Greg smiled, knowing all too well it could happen to anyone, even himself if he got caught cheating on Wanda. Cheating was an exciting thing to do, but it did have its risk.

"I really messed up this time," Alan said in a sad voice, "Judy doesn't want me to come back home." Alan hesitated then added, "I can't say I blame her." Alan was putting a backup plan into place in case Dawn would not have him at her place either.

"I see," exclaimed Greg, "so what are you going to do?"

"Well, the doctor said that I am supposed to rest for a few days before going back to work," Alan said with his friendliest smile, "and I was wondering and hoping if I could stay on your couch a few days, till I can find myself an apartment to rent and get back to work."

"Well, I'll have to ask Wanda," suggested Greg, but having Alan at their place for a few days would be fine with Greg. He liked Alan.

"You're a good friend," Alan sighed, "I really appreciate it."

"I'm a better friend than you think," Greg said as he sat in the big comfy looking chair next to the window. He was tired because Jeff had called early and woke him up.

"Oh, how's that," asked Alan, very curious now.

"Well, when I saw you and that pretty red head at the home show a few weeks back, and I did not mention it to Wanda," said Greg. "You know she's like a walking newspaper she would have told everyone." And he laughed as did Alan.

"You're right, I appreciate your discretion. I

remember you saying she doesn't keep secrets very well," Alan chuckled.

"Yes, you and I do have secrets in common don't we.," Greg recalled telling Alan about other women in his life.

"I'll see what Wanda says about you staying for a couple of days I think she'll be okay with it; she likes you. Come to think of it, she's not big on hearing about guys cheating on their women though." Then he frowned.

"Oh, that's not cool," agreed Alan.

"Tell you what, I'll use this phone and call her right now to see what she says about you staying for a few days," offered Greg. Greg was pleased that he caught Wanda at home. She was in a good mood but concerned about Alan and Dawn's conditions.

She had already talked to Dawn in the hospital. Wanda had sympathized with Dawn and said that she would kill Greg if he cheated on her. So Wanda is not happy and when Greg asked if Alan could stay with them a few days. Her immediate reaction was to tell him a flat out "no," but before she said anything more, she thought maybe it wouldn't be such a bad idea.

With Alan staying with them maybe she could use the opportunity get back at Greg and flirt with Alan a bit. Oh, she wasn't a dumb blonde, not at all, she could be just as conniving as the guys could be. She decided to use this opportunity to her advantage. She did think Alan was handsome, he had a good job, and he was probably soon to be a divorced man.

Greg insisted it would just be a few days, so she played it up and finally acted like she reluctantly agreed.

Alan was very happy to hear that Wanda agreed to let him stay at their place for a few days. Greg and Wanda were his backup plan. But he was hoping he could move in with Dawn. As soon as Greg left his room, Alan managed to get out of bed, put on his rob, grab a cane and slowly walk down the hall to visit Dawn in her hospital room.

Chapter Thirty-nine

"Dawn, how are you feeling," Alan asked in a low voice as he stood in the doorway leaning on the cane trying not to grimace with pain. He had just taken another pain pill and it hadn't quite kicked in yet. He stood slightly bent over in his hospital gown and loose-fitting robe. He had not shaved and his thinning hair was messed. He was trying to look pitiful so Dawn would feel sorry for him. It never occurred to him that lying all along to Dawn might have made her angry. He would not be getting a divorce if Judy had not initiated it. Alan still half-way expected he and Dawn would be together to heal at her place since he was about to become a single man. He thought that Dawn would be happy to know that they could then be together.

"I'm doing much better," Dawn said with a tone of confidence that Alan had never heard before, and it took him by surprise. She had changed somehow, gotten stronger, she wasn't that meek, quiet little girl anymore.

"Okay, if I sit down for a bit?" asked Alan slowly moving over to the comfortable looking chair near the window.

"Sure, have a seat." She figured she could give him a few minutes of her time.

"Don't tell me it's snowing again." He said in disbelief as he looked out the window before turning slowly to sit down.

"God, I hope not," complained Dawn, "I think only flurries are predicted."

"Looks like you are feeling pretty good." Alan made an attempt at conversation.

"Yeah, I'm doing okay," said Dawn trying to sound pleasant enough even though deep inside her heart raced with anger. She thought maybe it was better if he was sitting before she knocked him off his feet and took the wind out of his sails. She was angry that he thought he could just waltz right in as if nothing had changed between them, when everything had changed between them.

Dawn's plan was to make lots of changes in her life, and she would begin by ditching Alan. Next, although easier said than done, she planned on ditching her desires for flirty Nancy, who appeared to tease her just for fun. Dawn realized Nancy had no clue at all about how Dawn felt about her, so she had given up on her and turned her affections toward Judy. She made up her mind and planned to accept Judy's offer to stay at her house while her wounds mended.

Judy was warm, soft, and Dawn loved her kisses and the way her arms felt around her while holding her close. Judy had kissed her smack dab on the lips with long arousing kisses right there in the hospital. Judy brought out something in Dawn that had laid dormant and silent deep down inside of her for much too long. Being kissed by Alan was nothing like being kissed by Judy. Being kissed by Judy was warm and exciting and like flirting with forbidden fruit, and she loved it.

Being with Judy felt lovingly magical and spiritual and filled her heart with desire. She loved the tenderness and softness of holding another woman close to her body. She loved the sweet smell of her perfume, and the way her soft hands felt when they caressed her face and moved lovingly across her skin. She had desired Nancy, but Nancy never responded.

In a way Dawn felt she had to thank Ralph, Judy's father, for he had brought it all to the surface on that third night of the record-breaking historical Belleville Blizzard of 1982. She learned something very important about herself living with Alan. She learned for certain that she preferred women. She still wasn't ready to say the word lesbian and there was no need to. She smiled to herself thinking what a finale' to Three days and a gallon ofRosé.

Ralph had brought it all to a head. He had brought out the truth in everyone involved: Alan, Nancy, Judy and herself. Strange as it seemed, she felt an odd sense of gratitude for Ralph. Funny how it all came to be. If it wasn't for cheating Alan, she never would have met Judy.

In that respect Dawn had a certain soft spot for Alan, so she made an effort to speak nicely to him. He did look rather pitiful sitting there in that big chair wrapped in a shabby hospital robe with his unshaven face and messed up hair. She could see the bandages around his rib section through the gaps in his loosely tied robe.

"So, how are you doing, Alan?" Dawn asked trying to express a note of concern.

"Well, I am getting discharged from the hospital today," he said not really feeling like he should be discharged just yet. His mid-section was aching.

"I am getting discharged today, too," said Dawn

"That is great news," exclaimed Alan, "you look as if you are feeling pretty good. Are you?" he asked hoping she was better off than he, so she could take care of him at her place. He realized that was a selfish thought, but then again, he was a selfish guy.

"I'm not doing too bad," said Dawn. Actually she was excited about the prospects of staying with Judy. She imagined Judy crawling in bed with her and lying close with desire and making love. She felt excited, warm and tingling just by the thought of it. It actually took effort to bring her attention back to the man sitting in the big chair at the foot of her bed. She knew he noticed the faraway look in her eyes.

"Earth to Dawn. Where did you go," he wondered out loud.

"Oh must be these pain pills," Dawn lied with a smile not wanting to share what she was thinking and feeling. No way was she going to tell him about the fantasy she was having about Judy.

"Say, I thought since I'm about to be a free man, that I could stay with you," Alan said with his best sweet grin, "and we could take care of each other and heal together."

"Oh," Dawn responded slightly, but not totally surprised. It was just like Alan to think nothing of lying to her and cheating on Judy and then expect bygones to be bygones without remorse or any thoughts of asking for forgiveness. That was the least he could do, she thought. But, he cheated and lied, got her shot, and now expected her to take care of him, and that everything between them would go on as it had before all this happened. Dawn had seen another side of Alan and one she wasn't very fond of.

"What do you say?" Alan leaned forward in anticipation, eagerly awaiting her answer; he knew she would say yes. She was probably so excited she couldn't find the words to speak, he thought.

"I'm going to be staying with Judy," Dawn finally said. She couldn't resist telling him so matter of factly, just so she could watch his smile turn upside down into a frown. She saw the hopeful look fade and the sudden look of desertion and abandonment come into his lying eyes. She had to refrain from the urge to burst into laughter at the look of shock on his face. But she controlled herself and allowed only a small smirk to curve the corner of her lips he said he so loved to kiss. The look of disappointment on his face gave her great pleasure.

"Dawn," exclaimed Alan, "Judy is divorcing me!" He plainly said as if Dawn did not fully understand

"No shit," smiled Dawn speaking bold words in a

gentle manner, "well then, seems you're moving out and I'm moving in."

"But that can't be," Alan groaned a sorrowful moaning sound.

"Come on Alan, look at the bright side, at least we had our three days and a gallon of Rosé," Dawn was ready to put the past to rest and move on into the future.

And with that Alan felt it was no use talking any further to Dawn, so he slowly and painfully pulled himself up out of the chair, leaned on his cane and shuffled toward the door. It was plain for Dawn to see Alan was struggling with the truth of physical and emotional pain as he slowly hobbled out of her hospital room.

As he reached the hall, he passed a quizzically looking Nancy coming around the corner to the room. He said nothing but shuffled past her with his head down.

Chapter Forty

"Well, he didn't look good. What happened?" asked Nancy in a low concerned voice as she entered the room.

"Oh, just that the bullet he received was just a shot of reality, that's all I think," Dawn was rather pleased with herself. And here was Nancy back again to visit her, and Dawn wondered what was up with her. She could tell something was on her mind. Could Nancy actually be a little jealous that she had decided to accept Judy's offer.

"Well, he sure didn't look good," said Nancy. "I guess he did experience an awakening and found out that cheating on his wife can have its consequences.

"He wanted me to take him in and thought he and I could nurse each other back to health, " Dawn finally shared with Nancy, even though she had already put the past behind her. Alan was no longer her concern.

"You don't say," smiled Nancy. In a way Nancy was happy to hear Dawn wasn't fool enough to have Alan stay with her as if he hadn't lied and cheated on her.

"Yes, the audacity, if I must say so myself."

"I think you should move in with me," Nancy said.

Oops, Freudian slip, she meant to say stay with me for a while, but it came out differently than what she expected. Down deep did she really want Dawn with her after all, or did she want Dawn with her now that Judy had stepped in the picture? Nancy knew she needed to examine her own motives for wanting Dawn to stay with her.

"That's very sweet of you," Dawn replied. She wasn't sure what to think. Being shot had its awakening qualities. She had been feeling a little lonely and unloved. And now Alan with all his faults wanted her, Judy wanted her, and even Nancy wanted to take care of her. When it rains it pours, as the old adage goes. She actually felt blessed, and lucky too for not being shot dead. Ralph could have just as easily shot her in the head. She was filled with gratitude.

"Well, I want to take care of you," offered Nancy, "I care about you."

"Is Gerry okay with me staying with you?" Dawn wondered She was trying to feel out Nancy's true intentions. Dawn knew Nancy didn't like the idea of Dawn staying with Judy — but why?

"Oh, well, Gerry will be okay I think," Nancy's answer sounded doubtful even to herself.

Dawn wondered if Nancy thought she could have both Gerry and her and be intimate with both of them.

Nancy could tell by the look on Dawn's face that Dawn wasn't thinking too keenly about the idea. Down deep Nancy was jealous of Judy. Judy was pretty and sexy. Nancy wanted Dawn, secretly on the side, along with having Gerry as the main character in her life. It was a social thing with Nancy because the world frowned on same sex relationships. They were not socially acceptable and wasn't spoken of, and Nancy wasn't ready to face the many challenges that same sex relationships brought out into the public light.

What would people say? She was afraid she'd lose her status at work and with her friends. It wasn't worth going against the grain of social standards. Yet she had to admit to herself that she was jealous of Dawn having the courage to go to Judy's house and to stay with her because she loved her. Nancy could tell the way Judy had looked at Dawn, and Dawn at her, that there was a special connection between them. Nancy was jealous. She hated to admit it, but she was very jealous.

"Sure, well think about it," Nancy couldn't let go. "I have to go now. Call me, okay?" Nancy felt defeated. She was used to Dawn always saying yes to her invitations to go shopping, meet her at Panorama, or ride with her to Waterloo to visit her aunt and uncle. She knew she was going to lose that now and she did not want to.

"Okay, I will," smiled Dawn. She then looked past Nancy and saw Judy in the doorway. Her heart jumped. She watched as Nancy quickly turned, gave a quick hello to Judy, then slipped right past her brushing her shoulder as she rushed out of the room and ran down the hallway.

Chapter Forty-one

Dawn was being released and Judy had come to the hospital to pick her up and take her to her house.

"Take it easy now," suggested Judy, as she helped Dawn get out of her hospital gown and into sweatpants and shirt that Judy had brought for her to wear. Judy helped gather Dawn's things and she made sure that Dawn had her pain pills and all her personal items. She helped Dawn get into the wheelchair then wheeled out to the conveniently parked car. Judy eagerly and very carefully helped Dawn get into the car.

"I'll put your things on the back seat." She quickly kissed Dawn on the cheek.

"Ah, you are so sweet to me," smiled Dawn. Her heart was racing, not from struggling with the pain and trying to get into the car, but from Judy's kindness and her kisses. She was so in love with her.

"I'm happy to have you with me. I love you."

"I love you too," Dawn said almost shyly. She couldn't believe the love she had finally found. The mysterious feeling of love she had longed for so long and almost came to feel did not exist. She was elated and suddenly felt so much better just by being near Judy and looking into her clear blue eyes.

She could still feel Judy's soft sweet lips on her cheek. She felt as if she was in a love trance. Judy could have taken her anywhere and it would have been fine with her, just as long as they were together. Dawn would have had no qualms if Judy would have driven her to another state, another country, the moon or another planet. She would have happily and lovingly accompanied her anywhere. As it were, they headed down the road only a short distance to Judy's house.

Judy pointed out her dad's house as she pulled into her driveway. She reached up and pressed the button to the garage-door opener and stately double garage-door slowly opened. Dawn saw the vacant space for her car and that made her smile. Dawn felt that space was just reserved for her. She just knew that she would be staying long after her bullet wound healed and that she and Judy would be making a life together.

Judy helped Dawn out of the car and into the house. They came in through the kitchen door and Dawn's eyes grew big with excitement at the beauty and art features of the roomy kitchen. Dawn loved the layout of the open floor plan. The kitchen was situated where you could cook on the breakfast bar stove and look out into the open living room, something Dawn had only dreamed of having. The living room had a corner fireplace with huge ceiling-to-floor windows and large glass patio doors that opened to a huge patio.

The yard beyond the patio was beautifully

landscaped with trees and bordered with evergreens and shrubbery, making it a very private retreat area. The ranch style house was cleverly designed with the living room at the center and with the master bedroom and bathroom bordered on one side of the living room and two guest bedrooms suites on the other side of the living room. Judy showed her around, and then led her to the master bedroom where she softly kissed Dawn and gently led her to the big bed and carefully helped to lay her down. Dawn eagerly assisted as best she could as Judy removed her top, slowly, touching her gently near her wound.

"Does it hurt badly?" she asked kissing the area around the bandage.

"Not anymore," whispered Dawn as looked into Judy's loving eyes. She reached up and touched her lovely face as she totally surrendered to this lovely, loving woman. Being with Judy felt very natural, and Dawn felt at home in Judy's arms. Never in her wildest dreams had Dawn ever thought she could feel so loved and so moved. She wanted Judy desperately as Judy slowly finished undressing her and carefully, and tenderly made love to her kissing and caressing every inch of her. Dawn had never known such sexual excitement. Did she indeed die and go to heaven?

Chapter Forty-two

The next morning as Judy was preparing breakfast for Dawn, she was startled as her dad slipped in through the kitchen door.

"Dad, you scared the crap out of me," scolded Judy. "Are you trying to do give me a heart attack?"

"Sorry! Ah, breakfast," he smiled as he stepped closer to see, "is that for me?"

"Dad, come on, last time I saw you was when I visited you in jail," remarked Judy.

"That's true," admitted her dad.

"When did you get out?" She wanted to know.

"I was only there for a few hours," answered Ralph. "It helps to have friends in high places who owe you favors."

"I saw the newspaper article. You made the front page," smiled Judy said, knowing her father would have no trouble clearing up the mess his temper got himself into.

"Awful big breakfast for just one person," Ralph said looking around as if looking for another person. Judy didn't answer right away as she was busy watching the bacon fry and turning it ever so slowly.

Ralph took the liberty of slipping away and looking around the house. He headed to the master bedroom and peeked in. To his shock and amazement, he saw that woman who cheated on Judy with Alan, Dawn. She was sleeping. Ralph quickly turned around and hurried back to the kitchen.

"What's that woman doing here?" he demanded to know. Ralph always had a handle on his little girl. Judy knew he did not like her hanging around and sleeping with women, which was the very reason he found Alan for her. He thought Alan was her type, would straighten her out, so to speak, from her lesbian ways.

Ralph thought that Alan would be easy to control and therefore would keep Judy from such shenanigans. Oh, he wanted his daughter to be happy like every other father would want for his daughter to be happy; but Ralph was controlling and wanted to make sure his little girl was happy in a way that suited him. After he met Alan on the golf course at a Monsanto charity function, he introduced the two of them. Of course, he had not realized at the time that Alan was a philanderer. Alan was a little too much like he was himself, he came to realize.

Through their years of marriage Ralph had cheated on Susan numerous times. Ralph had no idea he made his wife sick with heartbreak and worry. She knew he cheated and figured her heartache probably led to her emotional downfall that brought on her illness and death. "I'm taking care of that woman because I

190

am very fond of her," confessed Judy with a tone that said, don't bother to say no, because she is staying right here with me.

"Right, come on Judy, you are as ruthless as I am," smirked Ralph, "and I know you well enough. I'd say you having her here is just a way of getting back at Alan."

"Come on dad you know that is not true," Judy pushed back in a stern voice, "I am not like you." She kept her voice lowered as to not wake up Dawn.

"Huh," he let out a sharp sound, "so we'll see." Ralph would rather have his daughter be as ruthless as he, rather than for her to have a woman lover in her life and in "his" house.

"She's a wonderful person," Judy said dreamingly, "I've never met anyone like her."

"Oh no, not since that girl in college you were fooling around with that I had to put a stop to." Ralph kept his voice low even though he felt suddenly very irate. This can't be happening again. He would not be disgraced all over again by having a daughter like that."

"I loved her," Judy was suddenly angry, and very sad. She had often thought about her love for her through the years.

"Huh," growled Ralph. In his mind he had determined that Judy would not embarrass him again. This will not happen again. He will not have important people in his life laughing at him again at the country club because his daughter was behaving in a queer sinful way. He was angry but said no more and abruptly turned on his heel and headed out the back door. What was he going to do? He worried and stressed as he walked back to his house. Too bad his aim was off—he could have killed both Alan and Dawn that night. He' would have to think of something now to get that woman out of Judy's life. There was no way he would stand for her audacious betrayal of behavior and subject him to the embarrassment of his daughter in a lesbian relationship.

Judy was upset about the way her father reacted when he saw Dawn in her bed. But she was not going to tell Dawn about what he said, how he behaved, or that he stormed out of the house. She only hoped that her dad was mad enough and would stay away for a while. She only wanted to be alone with Dawn. He could just stay away if he didn't like that she loved a woman. She wasn't a kid in college anymore. She had held back her feelings for women for years and she was not going to do it again. She had married Alan like her dad had wanted and her dad still wasn't happy. Her dad just needed to learn to mind his own business and get out of her love life.

Chapter Forty-three

Alan stayed with Greg and Wanda for a few days getting lots of rest on their surprising comfortable couch. While Greg was at work in the evenings, Wanda cooked good meals for Alan and managed to flirt with him a bit just to keep things interesting. But cheating again so soon and to a good friend was low on Alan's list; besides he was in physical and emotional pain and wasn't in the mood. Wanda flirtatious attempts did not go unnoticed, but they were not acted upon. He only played along and laughed it off as if she were merely kidding and joking around.

Greg and Wanda spoke with the apartment manager and helped Alan find an apartment in their complex. Within a few days they helped him move into a furnished apartment in the next building and helped him get the basic necessary kitchen and bath items. Wanda loved to decorate so she brought him some nice homey items. They gave him towels and bedding. Alan truly appreciated Greg and Wanda's help which helped lift his spirits and he was doing much better by the time he went back at work.

Soon he was back to working evenings and enjoying

his usual routine of stopping in at Panorama Lounge after work on his way home. Going back to Panorama was bittersweet for Alan, he enjoyed seeing his friends, but it seemed very strange without Dawn waiting there for him. He hoped Dawn was back in her apartment and away from Judy. He searched the parking lot for her car and searched the lounge for her. But to his disappointment she was never there, and this always made him sad. He needed someone to talk to, and he spotted Nancy at the bar. Alan thought she looked as miserable as he felt, so he made his way through the crowd up to the bar where she sat. Alan wanted nothing more than to commiserate with her. He was a bit nervous and not quite sure how she would greet him. Maybe she wouldn't even talk to him.

"Hi, Nancy, how are you?" He greeted her carefully. He searched her face for a friendly response. After all, Dawn was Nancy's best friend and he had lied and cheated on her too, not just on his wife. She could be very mad at him, but when she looked at him, she smiled a slight smile. He was glad to see her smile.

"Hi Alan, have a seat." She patted the unoccupied bar stool next to hers. She had been sitting there for a while with her space at the bar all staked out. She had her butt half sitting on the bar stool with a booted foot resting on the foot rail next to her purse and cash laid on the bar next to her lighter and half emptied pack of Tareyton 100s.

The barmaid just served up her second scotch and

water with a twist of lemon. She took a sip followed by a drag from her cigarette as she turned and looked Alan up and down. He seemed to be doing well enough she thought. She took another drag and ran her fingers through her natural blonde hair followed by an unconscious push to her glasses that had slightly slid down her lightly freckled nose.

She felt pretty and attractive that evening sporting a new white blouse and perfect fitting jeans. She owed her nice figure to the Jane Fonda workout exercise program she had been faithfully doing for the last year. And of course, playing racquet ball three times a week helped keep her fit and thin too.

She eyed Alan with an inquisitive stare. She herself wasn't quite sure how she felt about the whole situation with him lying to Dawn and telling her that he was divorced when he wasn't. Nancy had had similar experiences in the past with married men lying to her, once with a cop she dated who said he was divorced but wasn't, another time with an insurance agent who always claimed to be playing golf somewhere out of town every weekend so couldn't see her on weekends, when actually he was home with his wife and kids. So she had a sore spot for lying guys, but she was feeling a little mellow this evening after a couple of scotch and waters. Besides she wanted someone she could talk to about Dawn. So she was feeling extra generous and decided that Alan was an over-all nice guy. Besides, he looked pretty miserable with his ruffled hair and much needed shave. Nancy thought Alan looked like he wanted to talk and so she engaged him.

"Are you feeling better?" she asked him.

"Well, physically I'm okay," he hesitated then, not sure Nancy wanted to hear about his woes.

"Pretty shook up I guess. I know I would be if someone shot me."

"Well, I'm just sorry I messed up with Dawn. I miss her." He wondered did he really but convinced himself he did truly miss her. He was upset because he knew Dawn had had it with him. But what really bothered him was the fact that Judy took Dawn in, and that Dawn wanted to stay with her. He wondered if she played up to Dawn just to get back at him. Of course, he would think that he thought, he was beginning to realize just how self-centered and egotistical he truly was.

"Are you sorry?" asked Nancy. Just then she looked around at the doorway hoping it would be a while before Gerry showed up. She wanted to talk to Alan alone. Gerry was out drinking with his brother and his friends, or so he had told her; she was beginning to suspect everyone was cheating. Anyway, she hoped he was out with his brother and not with another woman cheating on her. She loved him but having been cheated on several times in the past, she always had that thought in the back of her mind. That came to the forefront whenever Gerry was late or had plans to go out with his brother and his buddies.

"You heard Judy took Dawn in," Alan asked in a

sad voice. He accepted Nancy's gesture for him to sit on the unoccupied stool she was saving for Gerry. She was glad when Alan sat down next to her and got right to the point. He was glad too that she was there being friendly and ready to talk to him.

He was careful to watch Nancy's reaction to his every word, he did not want to alienate their relationship. It was a complicated situation. He never dreamed Dawn would take up with his soon-to-be ex-wife. It would be a speedy divorce, because Ralph would see to it. Alan was sad to mess up his marriage, and lose their big fancy house and fancy country club status. But so far moving into a small apartment and losing his highfalutin social status was not too tough, and served him right for his bad behavior, he reasoned. Judy and her dad were all about show and looking upper class and Alan had come to enjoy to the better things in life. But now, Alan did not really care he knew he did wrong. Oh, well it's the price one pays for cheating on your wife. He was learning.

"Yes, I did hear that Dawn is staying with Judy." Nancy responded sharply. "And I can't believe it. I'm her best friend. I told her she should stay with me, that I would take care of her." She knew she sounded jealous but didn't care; truth be told, she was very jealous. She lit up another cigarette and puffed as she looked at Alan and waited to hear what he had to say.

"Well, I messed up, and I miss Dawn," remarked Alan taking a sip from his glass of wine the barmaid just sat in front of him. It tasted horrible! He almost spit it out. Suddenly he was sick of Rosé. It depressed him as it only served to remind him of the lovely three days and a gallon ofRosé that he and Dawn had shared. It seemed so long ago. The wine had left an unpleasant taste in his mouth and left nothing but visions of Dawn in his mind's eye. He had to push it aside and after catching his breath signaled for the barmaid to remove it and bring him a beer.

He missed the three days and the gallon ofRosé as Dawn lovingly referred to their stuck in the snow time together. Snow bound in her apartment, he had learned that he truly loved her. They had never spent three total days together; that is, until the big snowfall came and forced them together. It was what he needed to realize that he loved her. Those days seemed so long ago now and Dawn so far away.

He should have been jealous of Judy, but he didn't know how to put those emotions together. Did Judy really love Dawn, or was that Judy's way of getting back at him — to go after Dawn and take Dawn away from him. As it was, both of Alan's relationships were gone now. He was sad and sorry that he messed up, but he was not sorry of the time he and Dawn had spent during the snow days. Now Dawn was gone, and Judy was gone and the two ladies were gone together. He felt like the odd man out, and he knew it served him right. Who did he think he was anyway? Judy was teaching him a grand lesson and what got to him most of all was the fact that Dawn was so easily won over by Judy. How could she accept the affections of another woman over his? His ego was tripping him up badly. He took a swig of his beer and came back to the present when Nancy touched his arm to get his attention so she could commiserate with him.

"I miss her too," confessed Nancy sounding sad and near tears. I'm so used to her hanging out with me here while she waited for you to get off work.

"Hey, don't you start crying," warned Alan wiping his eyes. "You start crying I'm going to be bawling like a baby." And they both giggled through their tears.

It was hard to feel too depressed in such a festive place as the band was playing their 1976 hit "Disco Inferno," by the Tramps. It was one of those songs that you just had to get up and dance to. The band was playing, the crowd was happy and lots of people were dancing so Alan and Nancy got up and joined them. Dancing seemed to help lift their spirits. The lounge was crowded as usual and more friends were filing in, but for right now, Nancy wanted Alan all to herself so they could share in their misery. They expressed their shared grief for a few more minutes but were glad to see Dennis, Jeff, Greg and Wanda slip into a rare empty space they had found near them at the bar. Alan and Nancy only nodded to them in greeting.

Wanda could only guess what Nancy and Alan had talked about, or rather who they had talked about. She figured it was Dawn, since they both looked lost without Dawn sitting there between them.

The band had been on break and was returning to play another set. They had ended the last set with a favorite ABBA's "Dancing Queen" so now it was time to begin this set with a slow song.

"God, I hope the band doesn't play a sad song," said Nancy.

"Oh no, not 'Misty Blue,' by Dorothy Moore," moaned Alan. "That was our song," he said as couples began to move to the dance floor to dance slowly in each other's arms.

It was a sad sight for Alan to see, and he had to laugh to keep from crying. They managed somehow to keep talking and try to ignore the song. The music was loud, and the place was crowded and noisy, as great a distraction that could ever be, yet he was sad. And even though they were near a corner at the end of the bar, they had to get close together to hear one another and they were being shoved together anyway by passerby's. The place was small and popular especially when a popular band was.

"Well, I have to say that I am totally jealous that Dawn moved in with Judy," slurred Nancy after she waved to the bartender and ordered her fourth drink for the evening. She was planning on drowning her sorrows and spilling her guts to Alan. She made Alan swear not to tell Gerry what she was about to reveal. Alan downed his beer and motioned for another as if he was trying to catch up with Nancy. He promised as he crossed his heart and hoped to die pressing her on.

"I have a slight crush on Dawn myself," Nancy

confessed and surprised that she was not embarrassed to admit it.

"You do?" Alan asked, he was astonished to hear it.

"Yes, I do and I am not embarrassed to reveal it. Of course having three scotch and waters under her belt helped her admit it, and she had to laugh. She didn't care if he knew. She thought most women were bi-sexual and merely caved in to religious and social standards as to not rock the boat and to fit in and avoid embarrassment and fear of be ostracized from family and friends. Conformity was key to belonging to the group of friends, family, and co-workers no matter where you worked or what you did for a profession. She watched Alan smile at her slight booze enhanced confession.

"No kidding. Well, here's to love that got away from both of us," Alan said as he lifted his glass in a toast. They clinked glasses and drank up. Alan realized then that love is love, and of course Nancy hurt too just like he did.

"Well, I am sorry then that I moved in on you and stole her away from you." Alan apologized and meant what he said. He had learned a lot recently about loving and letting go of love.

"It is a mixed up, shook up world isn't it," Nancy almost feeling like crying. "We all love, and we all lose love at one time of another."

"You got that right," Alan was suddenly feeling like a wise philosopher. "I'm glad that you felt you could share that with me. Social norms stemming from religious teachings have a way of ruling our love lives, don't they? Either we pay attention to them or we don't and do what our hearts want us to do."

"I'm so glad you came in here tonight," said Nancy, "I just had to talk to someone and get this off my chest. Swear you won't tell Gerry."

"Your secret is safe with me," and he clumsily crossed his heart in a hope-to-die fashion. He and Nancy realized it was the second time he crossed his heart like that and hoped to die while he sat there and they both burst out laughing. At that point they were feeling no pain.

"I appreciate that," said Nancy as the band began to play "Brown Eyed Girl" by Van Morrison, a much happier song and one of their favorites.

"Hey, you know I can keep a secret, duh, being a married man that goes out on his wife. Of course, at the moment I am not real proud of my philandering ways. There was seriously something special between Dawn and me, and I learned that being with her those three days."

"Why yes I guess you can keep a secret can't you," said Nancy, "I sure didn't know that you were married."

"I'm not real proud of that, you know," Alan had to admit. It was true confession time since neither of them were feeling any pain having drank some of it away, and sharing heartfelt feelings helped. Then a thought popped into Nancy's head.

"Do you think Judy took Dawn in and is showing an interest in her in order to get back at you, Alan?" asked

Nancy. It was her last-ditch effort to make some sense out of the whole situation. She was full of questions. Alan did not reply at first and only shrugged his shoulders.

Looking sad he thought about what Nancy asked before he answered.

"Maybe," said Alan. "I thought that myself at first, now I'm not so sure."

"So what do you think about Judy's dad after all that you have been through?" Nancy was curious and couldn't resist asking. She was a little nervous about the fact that Judy's dad would use violence to get to Alan for cheating, and even go after the girlfriend who he didn't know at all. Such extremes, Nancy thought, and all to protect his daughter. Nancy wondered just what Judy's dad was capable of doing. Everyone knew Ralph Burns as an attorney who stretched the law at times or thought that he was above it. She knew that he was a powerful element in the community and heard that he was out of jail free of any charges.

"I think Ralph is a little crazy," shared Alan, "and it is hard telling what he might do next. I can't believe the jerk shot me and Dawn. Dawn was innocent. I feel bad for putting her in that position. It was wrong of me." Alan knew he should had known better than to get tangled up with Ralph Burns and his daughter, but he did not know at the time that Ralph was a controlling maniac.

Ralph controlled Judy like a puppet on a string, and he too after they were married. Money was power, and Ralph bought them many things including the house they lived in. He took them on expensive vacations all over the world. Of course, to most it all seemed like a lovely gestures but now Alan realized it was Ralph's way of controlling both of them.

Nancy was all ears, listening closely and glad that the band took a break, and she could hear Alan better. Alan went on to tell Nancy more.

"When we first met, Judy told me that when she was in college, she dated a girl. She said she was in love with her. Well, Ralph, her 'perfectly very conservative' dad, was not going to stand for his daughter having a lesbian relationship. Judy told me that he was worried about his reputation and insisted Judy stop seeing the girl because of the talk at his fancy country club. He was worried about his reputation."

"You're kidding," said Nancy and she was even glad to hear that Judy had had a relationship with a woman in the past to help legitimize her relationship with Dawn. Nancy was jealous and missed Dawn but still did not want Dawn to be hurt by Judy just trying to get back at Alan. So Nancy was glad to hear that Judy did have a college lesbian relationship. And in a way Nancy was glad too because, it would serve Judy's dad right for being such a prude. She wasn't sure that she was hearing Alan correctly with all the noise around them. But she caught the drift of it.

So Judy could be bi-sexual or a lesbian, she was even more surprised to think that Dawn was bi-sexual or a lesbian. She was suddenly sad at the possibility that she herself could have been with Dawn if only she would have come to terms with her own inner feelings. Actually, the thought was exciting to her. Oh, she had had experiences in college with women herself, but it just wasn't right then considering religious and social pressures. She didn't even like the girl at the time, even told her so. She knew now that she was in denial then and just protecting herself from ridicule and possible discrimination at work.

Were she and Dawn not admitting their feelings for each other all this time; they had spent so much time together? Were they more than friends? Nancy was intrigued and wondered about her own feelings for Dawn. Nancy realized that there may be a lot of same sex relationships going on if only it were religiously and socially acceptable. It appeared that people were afraid to talk about their hidden feelings about same sex feelings for fear of going against the grain. We as a society are brainwashed and controlled by restrictive religious powers that influenced government powers that are then extended and woven into the very thread of our social existence.

Nancy and Alan's conversation ended as Gerry arrived and managed to squeeze his way through the crowd and cozied up to them. Nancy and Alan's conversation was abruptly discontinued but not before they promised each other to talk again soon.

More folks came in and Alan, Gerry and Nancy were joined by Jeff, Dennis, Greg and Wanda who had also worked their way over through the crowd to join them. Everyone remained nice to Alan because they all understood. Things happen, and all is not fair in love relationships. Hearts get broken, people get hurt but they were grateful that Alan and Dawn had healed if not from their emotional wounds but from their obvious physical wounds. Alan received lots of hugs. Friends understood.

Chapter Forty-four

"Can I get you some more juice sweetie?" Judy sat on the edge of the bed and fluffed Dawn's pillow.

"You are so nice to me," Dawn said dreamingly. She never dreamed being with a woman could be so wonderful. She loved it. She loved Judy.

Judy took very good care of Dawn and was very attentive bringing her breakfast, lunch and dinner in bed for the first two days. Then Dawn insisted she need to get up and out of bed and move around more than just getting up to shower and use the bathroom. She insisted that she could get up and help Judy and eat with her in the dining room.

Judy was grateful she could check on her beauty salons from home. She was grateful that all was flowing smoothly and phone calls to get things fixed or repaired were easily handled either by her salon managers or herself without having to be there.

Dawn had been off work long enough and was going to have to get back to work as much as she got so used to being at Judy's. She loved being with her. Judy was so loving and tender, so she was going to miss all her wonderful attention when she got back to work.

"I love that you are taking care of me, "said Dawn and she kissed Judy, "but I have to get back to work." She watched a sweet smile slowly transform into a frown on Judy's sweet lovely face.

"No, I think it's too early for you to go to work," insisted Judy taking Dawn into his arms and holding her.

"I'm going to miss this," cried Dawn and truly meant it. She had found true love. And had no remorse for Alan or Judy's dad only love in her heart for Judy.

"I'm going to miss taking care of you," said Judy.

"So where do we go from here?" asked Dawn a little afraid of what the answer might be because she wanted it so much.

"Why not move in with me permanently?" asked Judy kissing Dawn and trying to persuade her she needed to be there with her.

"You want me here all the time, then," Dawn confirmed. Dawn was thinking that soon the lease would be up on her apartment, and she was going to have to make a decision anyway in a month or so. She loved being with Judy and if living with Judy was the way she was going to go, then she would have to make up her mind soon.

"You know I want you here," Judy said pulling Dawn close to kiss her.

Dawn was going to have to decide if living in this big house with Judy was what she wanted. Suddenly a little conservative lightning bolt of fear struck her heart, and she missed her friends. She knew they were all at the Panorama lounge almost every night partying like usual. All the things that had happened with Alan, Judy, and Judy's dad shooting her, really threw her for an emotional loop. Everything had suddenly changed. But right now, she had to plan to get herself ready in order to get back to work.

"I'm going to have to go back to the apartment and get some things for work." said Dawn, "Oh, my car is not here."

"Not to worry," said Judy, "take my car, we can get your car another time. I can't drive you there right now to get your things and your car, because I have to call back one of my salon managers to see if she got a plumbing problem fixed. I will probably have to be on the phone to work with them for a while until they get the problem fixed, so go ahead and take my car."

Dawn would have loved to stay in bed, but it was time to get up and get dressed and get ready to go back to work. So she took Judy's car back to her apartment to get some work clothes. She was all set then to go to work the next day. She had accepted a ride to work from a co-worker who lived in Judy's subdivision.

As Dawn drove Judy's car to her apartment her thoughts went over the last few days. She was mad about Judy. Judy was beautiful, sexy and warm. She loved being next to her, sleeping with her, and making love with her. The thought of living with Judy was exciting and intriguing, but at the same time it seemed that everything was happening so fast. The shock of Judy and her dad being at her apartment and getting shot, then finding out that Alan was married, and then his wife coming on to her like that was enough to send Dawn into a tailspin.

As it was, she was surprised that she was handling everything as well as she was. It all was so devastating to Dawn, and at the same time so wonderfully exciting. Judy ignored Alan completely that night and came to Dawn. Judy holding her and kissing her in the midst of the shooting threw her, so at first she didn't even know that she was shot. The police, the hospital and all that followed threw Dawn for a loop of emotions. She was star struck and crazy in love with Judy. Dawn was truly happy.

Dawn never allowed her heart to go for another woman, she ignored her feelings. Her heart could understand and sympathize with Judy when Judy told her that she had loved a woman in college, but her dad threatened not to pay her tuition if Judy insisted on continuing to carry on a sinful sick relationship with another woman. That story broke Dawn's heart as she could very well understand the torment as she herself had experienced the self-doubt and fear. Judy's dad had succeeded in making her feel little and ashamed of her love for another woman.

Dawn thought about Judy's story about her college love affair. She couldn't help but wonder just what Judy's dad would think of her and Judy being together if he broke up her college romance. Was Dawn in another dangerous situation involving Ralph? The thought scared her. It was obvious to Dawn that the man was a little crazy. After all he shot her and Alan, and he was out and about a free man and not in jail. Should she be worried, she wondered. He came after Alan and her because Alan was cheating on Judy.

Dawn could only hope that Judy's dad had a change of heart after all these years about Judy and lesbian relationships. Would Ralph come after her now for being in a lesbian relationship with Judy. Dawn decided she had some thinking to do; but she already knew she wanted to be with Judy.

Surely Ralph wouldn't do something stupid again. Hopefully, his police pals took his gun away from him. His local government official friends and fellow lawyers covered for Ralph and reported to the *Belleville News Democrat* that the shooting was an accident. Dawn felt better thinking that even Ralph had to know that it could not work twice. Another suspicious accident would not stand in the court of law no matter who Ralph Burns was or had been.

Dawn didn't want to think about all that right then, she was having fun and happy to be driving Judy's BMW, and to be on the way to her apartment to pick up a few things for work. She was looking forward to going back to work.

Chapter Forty-five

Ralph was angry and was not going to stand for his daughter being a lesbian, it was bad enough that she couldn't seem to live and act like normal Christian people do. It was difficult for Ralph to conceal his anger. His distractions were taking their toll on his business partner, their clientele and all their co-workers. They wanted to tell him to just get over it but were afraid of upsetting him more. They could see that he was falling apart. Ralph's co-workers avoided the coffee room as Ralph often stood in the small closet size break room doorway and blocked anyone from leaving, forcing them to listen to his tales of owe. He was driving them all crazy.

Chapter Forty-six

Judy was talking on the phone with the plumber who was working at one of her salons, when she spotted Alan at the back door.

"I came to get some stuff," said Alan, "I hope this is a good time."

"Okay, but I want you to go get your stuff and get out of here fast." Judy had sighed and covered the phone's mouthpiece, when she saw him come in the back door. She then went back to her phone conversation and ignored him. She was glad she was on a business call and did not have to talk to him.

Before Alan headed for the bedroom to get some of his things, he couldn't resist spouting off a bit to Judy. Old habits were hard to break when he was around Judy.

"Hey, I can't stay with Greg and Wanda forever," complained Alan.

"Well, you certainly cannot stay here," commanded Judy she was moving on with her life, a life without him in it.

"Why? It's my home too," Alan pointed out.

"Alan was playing Judy, he had already rented an apartment, but was working on Judy's sympathy.

"Oh please, you know its Dad's house," said Judy. "Everything about this house is all about dad," reasoned Judy. "Even me," she added with a negative tone that said things will change from now on.

"Actually. you are correct," said Alan knowing the truth all too well.

"So get your stuff out of here," insisted Judy. She felt nothing for him anymore. He could be a friend maybe, but that was beginning to feel doubtful, even though it was how she got to be with Dawn and Dawn was very dear to her.

Judy couldn't get out of her mind the image of Dawn's frightened face that night at Dawn's apartment and when she saw her crying and terrified. She instantly fell for her fragile emotional state. So wanted Alan out of there and gone and Dawn with her now. She had already made up her mind. Had she forced Alan to cheat on her because she was a lesbian, it's possible, but she doubted that. She felt it was the reason she couldn't really be mad at Alan for cheating on her with Dawn.

Alan finally got the message and began gathering his things. It did not take too long to fill up his little Volkswagen, and without a word he backed out of the driveway and drove away. It was time to begin a new life, and Alan was ready to move on. He had learned a lot in the past few years living with Judy and having her dad always there.

In a way he was rather excited, for who knew what the future held for him. He had time in the past few days after being shot and wounded to re-examine his life and how he felt about life and love. Why did he hop from woman to woman and cheat on his wife? Dawn wasn't the first he had cheated on his wife with, there were others. Was he searching for something deep within himself; his true self? He wasn't sure what it was but he was searching for something or someone to satisfy his soul purpose; for all the women he had been with left a void deep down inside; something was missing that he had not discovered yet. He was ready to begin his next chapter in life, and as he pulled away he imagined he saw Judy and Ralph both in his rearview mirror of past experiences.

Chapter Forty-seven

Ralph was becoming a serious drunkard. He even began drinking before work in the mornings pouring Irish whiskey in his coffee and taking a full flask of whiskey with him.

"Hey man, are you drunk?" Ralph's law partner Jim Hopkins asked with a stern tone one morning.

"No, I am not," Ralph responded, but there was no ignoring his own slurred voice and the clouds in his head. He could barely think straight.

"You can't sit in this meeting with our client in the state you are in." protested his partner. "You need to leave."

Ralph was not one to be told what to do, so after cursing his partner out, he left his law office in a rant slamming the door on the way out. His partner wanted him to leave, and that made him angry. In a heap of self-pity and domineering ego, he drove past the street to his home and instead went to Tim and Joe's bar and restaurant.

Many professional people from the St. Clair County courthouse, their clerks, secretaries, girlfriends, contractors went there for lunch and drinks and to meet for business dealings. It was a meeting place of professional connections. Ralph was so busy burning the ear drums of anyone who would listen to his crazy tales of woe of missing his wife and hating his son-in-law. Ralph Burns felt so above the law that he thought he could say anything about the night he broke into Dawn's apartment and shot Alan and Dawn, and nothing would happen to him. He was the law — he was a lawyer and in cahoots with every lawyer and judge at the St. Clair County courthouse.

"Scotch and water Tim," demanded Ralph with a slur to his voice as he bellied up to the bar. Ralph ignored Tim's cautious look that told Ralph he had already had enough to drink and needed no more.

"Think you might have already had enough Ralph," said Tim "how about having a Coke instead." As soon as he said it Tim could see that Ralph was going to throw a fit, but he set the bottle of Coke with a glass of ice on the bar in front of Ralph anyway — without the scotch and water.

"What the hell is this," asked Ralph glaring at Tim with anger in his eyes. He curled his fist ready to punch Tim for embarrassing him by making an ass of him, telling him he had had enough. The audacity! Ralph was high standing man in the community and no dumb bar owner was going to tell him what he should or should not drink.

"I think you have had enough," insisted Tim looking rather stern at Ralph. Ralph was a regular customer and until recently always behaved very professionally.

It was as if his alcohol consumption was catching up with him. He had not been acting rational ever since the shooting incident with his son-in-law. Recently Ralph Burns had been the topic of many discussions and conversations amongst the owners, waitresses and customers at Tim and Joe's, and they knew they were going to have to draw the line sooner or later if Ralph's behavior did not improve. They figured it wouldn't. Ralph had finally hit the last straw with Tim. He wasn't taking any more chances with Ralph—no matter who Ralph was or thought he was.

"I'll tell you when I have had enough, give me the scotch and water I ordered," Ralph demanded angrily. When Tim held his ground and did not turn to fix a scotch and water, Ralph picked up the bottle of Coke and threw it at Tim narrowly missing his head.

Tim being a bar owner for years had seen drunks like Ralph many times. He had suspected what was coming and thought fast. He wanted to protect his antique wall mirror behind the bar so when Ralph raised up and grabbed the coke bottle and pitched it at Tim. Tim in a lightning flash ducked his head, and quickly raised his arm to block the bottle from striking him. He had knocked the bottle to the floor where it crashed into pieces and Coke splattered all over the bar and onto customers who were sitting close to Ralph.

Embarrassed, Ralph turned, and without looking at anyone in particular, pushed his way through the crowd and stormed out the door. He staggered to his car parked in the parking lot. He was as angry as he had ever been. His mind was racing. He was mad at everyone. He had finally scared off Alan only to have his crazy daughter embarrass him further by taking in a woman, of all things. How could she do that to him? Judy took as a lover, the very woman her husband had cheated on her with, how crazy was that? Ralph was irate. He was going to put an end to this once and for all. He would not be the laughingstock of the community.

Ralph headed home, swerving from one side of the street to the other. He barely made it to his subdivision and nearly sideswiped a passing motorist as he turned onto his street. He stumbled into his house and called his daughter on the phone. He spoke to her in an ugly tone. He was trying to control her life as he had always done in the past. He could tell she was not happy to hear his voice.

"What do you want dad?" asked Judy in a serious tone not feeling like listening to her dad's complaints. His calls were usually filled with negative notations that degraded her day into a depressing mess.

"You need to get your head on straight," demanded Ralph speaking angrily to his daughter.

"Maybe you need to get your head on straight," Judy responded angrily for once. He was drunk and belligerent and she was tired of it.

"You can't speak to me like that, I'm your father," Ralph replied angrily. "I gave you life, and I can take it away."

"What?" Judy hung up on him; she had had enough of listening to this crazy man. The audacity! She couldn't believe her ears. She would disown him. She didn't need him. She ran three salons and was making great money. She didn't need him or his house. She had second thoughts about having Dawn move in with her in her dad's house. Maybe she should move in with Dawn or get another place they both could call their own.

She planned to discuss her plan with Dawn as soon as Dawn got back from taking her car to her apartment to get a few things for work the next day. Judy's dad's fits always drove her nuts, and her head began to throb with pain and worry, and it wore her out. Was her dad going off the deep end? She felt she had no control over her personal life. Her dad so wore on her nerves that Judy decided to lay down and take a nap and try to get rid of her headache till Dawn returned, and they could sit and discuss their next move.

Chapter Forty-eight

In a rant Ralph grabbed the gun from the living room lamp table drawer and stuck it in his coat pocket. He was not thinking clearing as he left his house. He only knew that he was mad. He was made at Tim at Tim and Joe's, he was mad at his partner, and he was mad at his daughter. He was mostly mad at his daughter. No daughter of his was going to talk to him like that, or behave like she was and embarrass him.

He managed to walk but stumbled most of the way up the block to Judy's house. He did not see her car in the driveway nor in the garage when he peeped in the window. He figured she had left to go check on her salons. He just knew that bitch Dawn was lying in bed in his and Judy's house—the house he bought for her. It discussed him that she showed no gratitude for all he did for her. He would punish her and get rid of that girl she had with her. Ralph was irate because unlike Alan who scared off most easily, his girlfriend did not and it made him mad that she was now with Judy. He wasn't going to have a cheating son-in-law in his life and he certainly was not going to have his daughter have a lesbian woman in his house or in her life. What would people think? He was a highly respected attorney in the county, at the Country Club and in the Catholic Church. He could not have this go on.

Ralph knocked on Judy's door and waited. Obviously she took the car and was gone. He decided that he wanted to take a look around and see where that other woman was, if she was still there on the mend with Judy taking care of her. He was mad. He should have finished her off that night when he had the chance. He wished his aim would have been better with both Alan and the girlfriend. He was mumbling as much aloud to himself as he stumbled around the outside of the house and sneaked around to the back and looked into the bedroom window.

That woman, that lesbian woman, was still there in Judy's bed. Judy was still taking care of her. Ralph grew very angry in his drunken stupor when he saw her lying there. He had had three quick shots of whiskey at his house before walking up the street and his head was buzzing. He was going to have to set some new rules. He quietly unlocked the back door, slipped through the kitchen, down the hallway and peeked into the master bedroom. It took a while for his eyes to adjust from bright daylight to the dimness of the house. He was staggering and bouncing off the walls and made a racket that woke Judy up lying under the covers in the bed. She turned and halfway raised up under the covers.

"You ..." Ralph saw the movement in the bed, reached in his pocket and pulled out his revolver and shot. He shot Judy squarely in the forehead. Judy was dead and then Ralph realized the horror of what he had done.

"No! Oh hell," he screamed and staggered against the wall then took a few steps forward. He let out a mournful yelp that sounded like a wounded tortured animal. He burst into tears when he realized he had shot and killed his very own daughter. What had he become? His head was full with grief, sorrow, guilt, shame and self-hatred. He had gone too far this time. Judy lay lifeless in the bed. Bright crimson red blood oozed everywhere and soaked the white pillows and sheets. Ralph saw the horror of it and dropped to his knees, moaning in agony.

"What have I done, what have I done?" he cried. The pain was too much. The revolver was still in his hand. He looked at Judy, looked at the gun, then slowly and deliberately put the revolver to the side of his head and pulled the trigger. His lifeless body slumped to the floor.

Chapter Forty-nine

Alan was upset after speaking with Judy. She had given him a limited time to get his stuff out of his and Judy's home. He drove to his apartment, emptied the Volkswagen and put all the stuff away. Then realized he had left some things he needed under the bed. He needed to make another trip back to the house and get those things, so he got in his car again and headed to Judy's.

He had time to think as he drove to Villa Hills from his apartment in Swansea. He wondered if his wants and desires for extramarital affairs and excitement had messed up his life and those around him. He had spent the previous evenings again speaking with Nancy about it. She sympathized with Alan and in so doing had to take another look at her own relationship with Gerry.

Chapter Fifty

Nancy's talk with Alan at Panorama the night before had her wondering if she was really in love with Gerry? Gerry was sound of mind, as far as she could tell, grounded and would be a faithful partner for her. But something was missing. She had come to the realization that the touch of a woman was missing, and just the thought of it made her heart ache. Lately Nancy found herself visualizing and thinking about Dawn as she and Gerry made love.

She hesitated to share this with Alan as they sat at the bar at Panorama Lounge. It was just weird that Dawn was not there with the "group" as the gang referred to themselves. It was just not the same without Dawn's conversations that were filled with jokes, laugher and sly remarks.

"Thanks for meeting me Nancy," said Alan, I'm glad we got together this evening. I needed someone to talk to." Alan sat on the bar stool next to Nancy. He sipped on a beer and she sipped her usual scotch and water with a twist of lemon.

"You like lemon in your scotch and water," Alan commented, never really seeing that before.

"I always get a lemon twist in my scotch and water. Dawn would be so mad when the bartender would also put a lemon twist in her scotch and water. She didn't like it in hers," Nancy laughed.

"You miss her too, don't you?"

"We both smoke Tareyton 100s and she would get so mad if she mistakenly picked up my cigarette instead of hers out of the ash tray. She said she knew right away it was mine because the tip of my cigarette was always wet," Nancy smiled remembering. "She would ask 'just how do you smoke that cigarette to get the tip wet like that?'" Thinking of it made Nancy sad, and she missed Dawn.

"It's the little things isn't it?" Alan sighed.

"Yes, it is," replied Nancy with sadness in her voice.

"Dawn never cared for the smell of cigars," said Alan.

"Well, that I can totally understand," laughed Nancy. They chatted and were soon joined by the rest of the group as the evening went along, dancing and having a great time. Everyone asked them if they heard how Dawn was doing.

Chapter Fifty-one

Alan thought about his conversation with Nancy the night before. He was thinking of Dawn when he pulled into Judy's driveway at the same time Dawn pulled up in Judy's car. At first Alan thought it was Judy. His heart took a leap when he saw that it was Dawn getting out of Judy's car. They quickly and uncomfortably greeted each other before going into the house.

"How are you feeling Dawn?" asked Alan with mixed feelings. Things had changed between them since Ralph shot them both. It was like a new reality had set in. It had given them both time to think and examine their lives and their true feelings for themselves and other people in their lives.

"I guess I'm feeling much better now, thanks for asking," Dawn had reverted to politeness but still harbored hurt feelings. After all, Alan did lie to her about being married. She could have been killed, and she was innocent thinking she was dating a single man.

"Look, I'm sorry for all that has taken place." Alan said sincerely.

"Well, what can I say, we're both alive," said Dawn,

"and I'm moving in and you're moving out. Like revolving doors, I guess." She added with a snippy tone.

The front door was locked so Dawn used her key. Alan was right behind her when she went into the house. The house was quiet like no one was there.

"Judy," Dawn called out as she flipped on the living room lights, headed for the kitchen. Something felt odd and strange. She could tell that Alan felt it too. There was an eerie feeling about the house, as if something there was terribly wrong. With knots in their stomachs they silently and slowly walked down the hallway toward the master bedroom where they came upon the horrific bloody scene.

Dawn and Alan both screamed and cried at the dreadful sight that laid before them. Ralph Burns was dead on the floor in a pool of blood near the doorway to the bedroom. It was plain to see he had shot himself in the head as the gun was on the floor next to him. They looked in the doorway and saw Judy dead in her bed. She had been shot int the forehead. It was plain to see what had happened, Ralph had shot her and then shot himself. Dawn and Alan both gasped at the sight. Dawn nearly fainted and Alan caught her and held on to her as she screamed and burst into tears. Alan held her close as they both sobbed.

"My god, what has that crazy man done?" Alan cried. All he could do was hold Dawn, as she was shaking and sobbing violently.

Chapter Fifty-two

The next few days were very hard for Dawn. Alan tried to be of some support and some comfort. But Dawn had mixed feelings. She was confused. Circumstances with Alan had Dawn meet Judy, and she got to be with her for a wonderfully magical although very short time.

Alan did not want a double funeral for his wife and her dad. But somehow the mortuary put Judy in one parlor and Ralph in the next parlor at the same funeral home. It was very difficult for everyone who attended. Alan stood next to the coffin with a few of Judy's distance relatives who came to pay their respects. Some clients and all the hair stylists from Judy's three beauty salons came to offer condolences.

Dawn stayed more in the back corner of the parlor preferring to be by herself. Nancy came in with Gerry and they stood and talked to Alan and Wanda and Greg. After speaking with Alan and a couple of the ladies who worked in the salons. Nancy looked around for Dawn and Wanda pointed her out. Nancy saw that she was sitting all alone by herself in the back of the parlor. Wanda and Greg had spoken briefly with her before Dawn retreated to the back of the room. Wanda warned Nancy that Dawn was very shaken. Nancy left Gerry talking to Greg and Wanda and walked over to Dawn who stood up when she saw Nancy coming her way and reached out to her. Dawn cried as Nancy held her in her arms for the longest time. They both cried.

"Thanks for being here," said Dawn, "it means a lot to me. "She sobbed than added. "I loved her a lot. She brought out something in me that was very important, that I never allowed to happen before. She was a gift."

"I know sweetheart. I'm here for you," said Nancy as she held Dawn close. "Society has a way of not allowing us to bring forth our true selves. Social 'norms' many times do not allow us to really be who we are… we need to change that." Nancy backed away far enough to hold Dawn face in her hands and kiss her tear stained cheeks very tenderly. Dawn closed her eyes and realized that Nancy would always be there to hold her close.

Chapter Fifty-three

Weeks passed and Dawn had settled back into her work routine living comfortably in her apartment. She enjoyed time with the "group." Her most cherish time however was one on one time with Nancy when they went shopping or visiting Nancy's aunt and uncle in Waterloo for barbecues and playing card games on Saturday afternoons. Nancy and Dawn had been to Panorama but had not seen Alan. Nancy had heard from Gerry that he was busy getting things in order after Judy and her dad's funeral.

Alan sold the big house that he and Judy shared. He sold it cheaply to Judy's relatives. He just wanted out of it. It was just too big and there were just too many memories. Some good and some of which he just felt guilty about. Two people were dead because he could not remain faithful to his wife.

Alan still felt that Judy came on to Dawn just to get back at him. Of course his self-centered ego would think that. The "group" still sees Alan once in a while. He usually comes to Panorama Lounge after working evenings when he gets off work at eleven. He looks forward to seeing Dawn there, as does Nancy. Nancy is well aware how Alan feels about Dawn, but all remain civil and glad to be alive. There was an unspoken competition between Alan and Nancy when it came to Dawn, but finally Alan gave up.

He realized it was more his pride than anything. He was falling back into his old habits and did not like it. He saw a psychologist to get his head straightened out, and oddly enough what came out of his counseling sessions was he may be a latent homosexual. That was the reason why he moved from woman to woman. Finally, it all made sense to him. Was there something in the air, something in the water? Were there lingering electrical charges remaining in the air from the thunderstorm blizzard? Were they all coming out of the closet?

Dawn and Nancy became an item. It took time for Nancy to realize Dawn was what she wanted and not Gerry. Gerry and she had dated nearly a year. It was a sad day for him when Nancy confessed one morning that Dawn had spent the night with her. He wanted to know why Dawn instead of him.

"You brushed me off last night," complained Gerry," I always followed you home from Panorama, now you are making time with Dawn."

"Yes, it appears so," admitted Nancy, "I'm sorry but truth be told I have always loved her and was merely trying to fit in with the expectations of the straight world."

"Well, can't say I blame youfor living your truth." Gerry had recently done a little soul searching himself and was all about love being love, and being happy was the most important thing in life. Stop trying to please the world and please yourself.

Chapter Fifty-four

Dawn and Nancy spent lots of time together now whenever they could. It was the end of February and another big snowstorm was promised for their area.

"Why don't you come over here," suggested Nancy, "I have beef stew cooking in the Crock Pot for us and it's a lot, enough to last three days if you bring the gallon of Rose' '"

"Here we go again: Three days and a gallon of Rose'. Very funny," laughed Dawn, "Okay you're on, I'll bring the gallon of Rose'"

"I'm excited," exclaimed Nancy

"I am too, I hope it snows a lot," laughed Dawn.

Chapter Fifty-five

It did snow but not another record snow fall. Nancy and Dawn, slept late in each other's arms. Dawn stayed for more than three days and a gallon of Rose'. She moved in with Nancy when her own apartment lease was up that following month. They still met up with the group at Panorama and at Jeff and other's house parties. They gave a couple of parties themselves.

Talk at Panorama was that Gerry and Alan were hanging out a lot together. Although they would never admit to anything gay between them. The group was open to it however, just as they were open to Nancy and Dawn being together.

Love is love and one should go where the heart is. Life and love are precious and wonderful loves may come once in a lifetime. Don't marry someone just because your father thinks the man is right for you or would be embarrassed at the Country Club just because you love someone of the same sex. Life was filled with surprises and revelations.

At the double funeral for Judy and her father, Dawn learned that Ralph had a secret relationship with his law partner Jim Hopkins when they watched the man cry uncontrollably and hug the closed coffin. The law partner had attended the funeral in tears and poured his heart out in front of his wife and everyone. It was just too bad that Ralph was so homophobic.

"May he rest in peace, finally," said a weeping Jim Hopkins his law partner and secret lover. Ralph was very homophobia, Jim said he had wanted to come out to everyone about him and Ralph. But Ralph had had a bad experience as a young man when his father caught him and another young man having sex in Ralph's bedroom one afternoon. It messed him up badly, Jim said. And now with all the television coverage about AIDS (Acquired Immune Deficiency Syndrome) epidemic all the time and the hatred for gays, Ralph would never come out of the closet.

It was 1982 and many gay men were dying of AIDS and Ralph was full of fear and shame. No one acknowledged the AIDS epidemic in government until after Reagan as elected and the First Lady, Nancy Reagan's hairdresser was gay. She sympathized and pushed for legislation so that medication was introduced.

AIDS was officially recognized on June 5, 1981 when the CDC (Centers for Disease Control and Prevention) published a clinical article and acknowledged five young males who were infected.

Time went on and Nancy and Dawn were very happy, they even ventured back to Lill's with another couple in toll, oddly enough that couple was Alan and Gerry. There was another gay bar now, across the street from Lill's, called Buff's. The places were very popular with bands and dancing. Buff's had an eleven o'clock drag show every Thursday night, and Alan and Gerry dared to participate after some encouragement from Nancy, Dawn, Greg, Wanda, Dennis, Deb, and Jeff and the rest of "the group" who attended and cheered them on.

Many times Dawn, Nancy, Alan and Gerry call themselves the odd couples and laugh. But mostly they wondered had the magnetic electrical charges in the thunder and lightning effected their own electrical systems and sparked the changes that were made in each of them.

"Yeah, but Greg and Wands are still a straight couple," Alan pointed out adding, "evidently the frequent strange thunder and powerful lightning that occurred during the blizzard didn't change them."
"Oh yeah, so why is Greg staring at the tall blonde guy, that I could easily go for myself?" Wanda worriedly wanted to know. She looked around and the rest of the group only shrugged their shoulders and smiled.

But they all agreed as the Phil Collins song goes — there was definitely something in the air that night — as hearts were turned during the record-breaking blizzard of 1982.

Alan and Gerry, dressed in drag, wowed the crowd with their cooked-up song dance routine to "I Got You Babe," by Sonny and Cher. Everyone loved their routine and applauded.

Dawn congratulated Alan when he and Gerry

finished their song and dance. They hugged each other remembering their time together but both feeling like they are where they need to be now.

"Here's to us and our new loves," Alan smiled.

"And here's to our Three Days and a Gallon of Rose," replied Dawn as they clinked their wine glasses together.

About the Author

This is Dianne Zimmermann's fourth novel. Her other books are *Emma's Run, Jane's Aliens, Hooch Runners,* and *Pleasant View* were published by BookCrafters. Dianne lives in St. Louis and enjoys writing, drawing, photography, running, hiking and road trips.